Better-off Bunny

Hey There, Hop Stuff

Book 1

Cover artwork by Gombar Sanja.

https://fantasybookcoverdesign.com/

Interior artwork by Cauldron Press.

http://www.cauldronpress.ca

A huge thank you to-

Allison Woerner for Alpha Reading

Maxine Meyer for Copy Editing.

Imogen Evans for Proofreading & Editing.

BETTER-off Bunny

1
HEY THERE, HOP STUFF

SEDONA ASHE

CONTENTS

Chapter One   1
Chapter Two   9
Chapter Three   15
Chapter Four   21
Chapter Five   27
Chapter Six   33
Chapter Seven   39
Chapter Eight   45
Chapter Nine   51
Chapter Ten   57
Chapter Eleven   63
Chapter Twelve   69
Chapter Thirteen   75
Chapter Fourteen   83
Chapter Fifteen   89
Chapter Sixteen   95
Chapter Seventeen   101
Chapter Eighteen   107
Chapter Nineteen   113
Chapter Twenty   119
Chapter Twenty-one   127
Chapter Twenty-two   135
Chapter Twenty-three   141
Chapter Twenty-four   147
Chapter Twenty-five   157
Chapter Twenty-six   167
Chapter Twenty-seven   173
Chapter Twenty-eight   181

About Sedona Ashe   189

Chapter ONE

CILLIAN

"Would it kill you guys to eat breakfast at a different restaurant occasionally?" Brett huffed, annoyance written in the frown lines on his face.

"Stop whining. You are free to eat wherever you want. No one is forcing you to tag along with us every day," Syrus mumbled. He tried to appear gruff, but there was no missing the sparkle in his dark brown eyes as the restaurant in question came into view.

And Syrus wasn't the only one affected by the nearness of the little café. My heart pounded hard against my rib cage.

"I don't understand your fascination with that place. The food is subpar, and I swear I'm allergic to the rabbits who own it. My nose is already itching just thinking about it." Brett rubbed his nose. "I'd love to eat somewhere else.

Heck, the only reason I come along with you guys is so that we can get the morning reports out of the way over breakfast."

Rig's brow wrinkled, and his lip curled. "I'm sick of doing the reports while trying to enjoy my meal. Let's schedule fifteen minutes in the office after breakfast each day to go over them."

Nodding in agreement, I waved Brett away. "I agree. Go eat wherever you prefer. Meet us at the office afterward, and we will set aside time to go over your documents before we start replying to emails and returning calls."

Looking down at the overflowing manila folder in his hands, Brett hesitated. The loud rumble from his stomach helped speed up Brett's decision, and with a sigh, he stuffed the folder back inside his briefcase. "Fine. I'll grab a break-fast burrito across the street. I'll see you guys at the office."

We didn't respond as he walked away. Our attention had been captured by the radiant beauty who'd emerged from the tiny café with a steaming pot of coffee in each hand.

"Monroe." Syrus breathed her name.

She was elegance in motion as she weaved between the bistro tables, refilling coffee mugs. Her smile was so genuine that even the grumpiest of guests couldn't help but return her smile.

"It's like she glows." Rig's hushed voice was reverent as she stopped at a table of crying kids and worn-out parents. "Watch how they respond to her."

He wasn't wrong. The diminutive waitress spread

sunshine while working her way through the guests, filling the caffeine-deficient parents' cups and pulling giggles from the impatient toddlers. A few minutes later, when she moved away from the last table, every diner, young or old, wore a bright smile. The waitress's positive energy was contagious.

"Are we going to talk to her today?" Syrus chewed his bottom lip, a sure sign that he was anxious. "We've been visiting this place for three months and have yet to say more than a few sentences to her. For all we know, she already has a boyfriend."

At the word *boyfriend*, every muscle in my body tensed. Rig's low, menacing growl let me know he felt much the same way.

Speaking through clenched teeth, I tried to be the voice of reason. "We haven't smelled one particular male scent on her consistently, so it's unlikely she's bonded to anyone. But we need to remember that even if she is single, she's probably not going to be interested in us as potential mates."

"Because we're wolves," Syrus whispered, his shaggy blonde hair covering his face as his gaze dropped to the ground.

"Yeah. That." My words were clipped. You would think being a wolf shifter would be a point in our favor, but in this case, it definitely wasn't. All because the energetic beauty who'd captured our hearts, and starred in all our dreams, was a rabbit shifter.

A bunny.

And although that fact didn't bother our wolves in the

slightest, it was likely to cause some issues for Monroe. Wolves and rabbits often frequented the same businesses, but we never hung out socially in the same circles. The rabbits had also chosen not to attend the same schools and colleges as wolf shifters.

From what we'd been told, a rabbit could never feel completely relaxed while in the presence of wolves. It was a deep-seated survival instinct that had the rabbits on constant guard around predators.

Sure, tolerating us for an hour while we ate in a public place near them was doable, but asking Monroe to close her eyes and sleep while surrounded by a pack of wolves might never be possible. What if we convinced her to be with us, and it caused her to be under constant stress? Long-term, the anxiety could take a toll on her body. I was determined to figure out a way to take away any fear of wolves she might have.

My chest rumbled, echoing the pain I felt in my heart. I wanted her to be mine. *To be ours.* Werewolves don't have fated mates. Instead, our wolves choose a mate for us. Rig, Syrus, and my wolf had selected the same mate—an adorable, raven-haired waitress.

She was meant to be our bunny; I just hadn't yet figured out how to convince her we could make a relationship work between us.

"It would probably make sense to talk to her and see if she is even open to the idea," Rig said from beside me. He must have picked up on my train of thought through our bond.

4

I blew out a long sigh. "You're right. Although, at this point, I think it's too late for us to walk away from her without getting our hearts broken." Running a hand down my face, I added, "Let's do it. It's time to talk to her."

Syrus's head snapped up, and a thousand-watt grin spread across his face. "Yes! It's about freaking time."

He didn't speak again as we moved through the white picket gate that led onto the café's dining patio. Good thing, too, since I was still trying to decide whether I'd lost my mind. What if I was wrong? Was this really the day for us to do this?

Monroe whirled on her heel, turning to face us. Her beautiful, heart-shaped face stole my breath. "Good morning! Take a seat wherever you like, and I will be right with you." Without waiting for a response, she bustled through the side door of the quaint restaurant and disappeared inside.

Each table was covered in a white tablecloth and adorned with freshly cut flowers. After a quick scan, I spotted a lone table in the back corner of the patio. Giving a quick jerk of my head, I signaled for Syrus and Rig to follow me.

Today was the day we were going to try to talk with Monroe, and I hoped it would be easier to strike up a conversation with her if we weren't sitting smack in the middle of the tables. Plus, I preferred having my back against the railing; it allowed me to keep an eye on the rest of the patrons who pretended not to notice us. I hadn't missed how every back had straightened, and the conversations had become hushed as the diners caught our scent on the wind. They knew we were wolf shifters, and it had them on edge.

We'd barely settled onto the pale blue cushioned seats before Monroe reappeared. Three cups and large plates filled with scones balanced precariously on her oversized serving tray.

"Good morning, gentlemen! How are you on this fine day?" As Monroe spoke, she placed a steaming mug of black coffee in front of me, a foamy latte in front of Syrus, and a cappuccino by Rig's plate.

My heart gave a ridiculous flip. She'd remembered what we liked. Logically, I knew she probably remembered what drinks all her regular customers preferred, but my wolf was convinced this proved we had a special connection.

"Would you guys like to hear today's specials?" Monroe pulled a tiny purple notebook from her apron pocket and flipped it to a clean page. She nibbled on the end of the pencil as she met our gazes around the table.

"Yes, please." Syrus rested his chin on his palm, staring up at her like a lovesick Labrador pup.

I barely held back a snort. Syrus ordered the exact same thing every time we came here, but he wasn't going to miss an opportunity to listen to her sweet voice.

Monroe rattled off the daily specials, the corner of her mouth turning up in a small smile when we each ordered our usual dishes.

Unable to hold it together for another second, Syrus blurted out, "Do you have a boyfriend?"

Rig buried his face in his palm, and a muffled groan came from behind his hand.

I choked on my coffee and spluttered at the younger wolf. "Smooth, Syrus. Real smooth."

Syrus's tanned skin turned the deepest shade of maroon I'd ever seen.

Monroe had been in the process of tucking the sticker-covered notebook back into her apron pocket, but at Syrus's question, she missed the pocket of her apron, and the tiny notebook tumbled to the ground.

"What?" she squeaked, and her skin bloomed with a deep blush that nearly matched the current shade of Syrus's skin.

Leaning to the side, I reached for the fallen notebook, intending to hand it to her. Instead, Monroe had leaned down at the same moment, and our heads banged together with a hard thud.

"Ouch!" Monroe yelped.

Unable to help myself, I caught her face in my hand, tilting it gently to each side so I could inspect her forehead. This was the first time I'd ever touched her skin, and I was amazed by how soft it was—far softer than any flower petals I'd ever touched.

My gaze traveled to Monroe's mouth. Would it be just as soft? Before I could think better of it, I brushed my thumb across her plump pink lips. To my shock, she sucked the tip of my thumb between her lips, and the velvet of her tongue slid across my rough skin.

In an instant, my body grew harder than stone. It was a

simple gesture, and yet it was the most sensual thing I'd experienced in my life. My wolf whimpered with need, and I gave a low groan.

Monroe's body jerked as though she were coming out of a daze. With a gasp, she reeled back on her heels. Stumbling to her feet, she murmured something intelligible about the kitchen and orders before rushing inside the café.

"I'm fighting the urge to kill you right now." Rig snarled, his breathing rough.

"That was the hottest thing I've ever watched. Just imagine having her in our bed." Syrus's eyes sparkled, and his cheeks flushed, this time from lust rather than embarrassment.

I sat up in my chair, my eyes drifting to the door she'd disappeared through. My lust quickly turned to lead in the pit of my stomach. Monroe had been scared, and then she'd done what her nature drove her to do. She ran. How could it ever work between a bunny and a wolf?

Chapter TWO

MONROE

I fanned my flushed cheeks and sagged against the kitchen wall. Why, for the love of pepperoni pizza, had I licked that man's finger? Worse—and yes, this was worse—it hadn't been just a random man's thumb. Nope. It belonged to *him*. Cillian. The man who could never be mine. Just like I couldn't ever consider a life with Syrus or Rig.

At the thought of Syrus and Rig, my face burned as though it'd been torched by the sun. What did they think of me now? Probably that I was living up to the most exaggerated reputation of rabbit shifters.

There wasn't a rabbit shifter on earth who hadn't heard the rumors the other paranormal species spread about us. To be fair, the gossip held a bit of truth, and the phrase 'breeding like rabbits' wasn't too far off the mark. Where most people were misinformed was when they believed the claim that all rabbits were nymphomaniacs.

Wrong! That only applied to the females among my species. We were basically the succubi of the shifter world. This was why each rabbit shifter female had to be paired with a group of males. It was the only way to keep the females sated and the males from being bred to death. Although, I'd heard it wasn't the worst way to go.

The elders had created the harem setups among rabbits almost a hundred years ago, and since then, there'd been far fewer sex-related deaths in the burrows. Unfortunately, it had created other issues... the type of issues that made it impossible for me to express any interest in the three sexy wolves on the patio. Which made my slip-up even more of a problem.

I decided to blame the nearness of spring. Female rabbits had their first heat between the ages of twenty-one to twenty-five. After our first heat, we came into heat every eight to twelve weeks. Those were the weeks we were especially fertile and overly needy.

The first heat of every spring was the most uncontrollable for all female rabbits, and it was second only to what we had to endure during our very first heat. The truly sucky part was that every female rabbit's first heat coincided with the first heat of spring. It was a double whammy and created the most painful, but also most erotic, experience in a rabbit's life.

To prevent issues, rabbit females had their blood drawn regularly to ensure they were matched with their fluffle, a.k.a. harem, before the first day of spring. I turned twenty-three last month, and my blood work had shown a spike of hormones that indicated my first heat would happen this spring.

My eyes darted to the calendar on the wall, and my heart sank. There were only three days left until spring. Every last ounce of happiness drained from my body.

As a young girl, I dreamed of growing up to be exactly like my mother and dedicating my life to being a good mate and mother. I'd thrived on the energy, love, and joy that existed in my family. That was all destroyed the day coyote shifters attacked the rabbit burrows. They'd slaughtered over a hundred rabbits in a matter of minutes. Because violence between shifter species was rare, it made the coyotes' vicious acts even more shocking.

The wolves had come to our defense, driving the coyotes back into the depths of the forest. Thanks to the brave wolf shifters, hundreds of rabbits were saved, but it was too late for my parents and siblings. My family had perished, leaving me the lone survivor. While my body was uninjured, my memories bore traumatic scars. I knew I'd never be able to get the smell of coppery blood or the shrieks of dying rabbits out of my mind.

My life changed in every way possible that day, becoming far different from what it had been before the attack. I'd been taken in by a sweet older fluffle who'd been unable to have children of their own. They loved me, and with time, I'd grown to love them back. But they had been snubbed by most of the community and were considered outcasts due to never producing children for the burrows.

This attitude had extended to me, and I'd learned the hard way it was best to avoid rabbits of my own age. Bunnies may be adorable, but they are also vicious.

With each passing year, being bonded became something I dreaded rather than something I looked forward to. I'd resigned myself to being matched, only because there wasn't another option for female rabbits. I knew my fluffle was likely to be loveless, but at least I'd survive my heat. And after I produced a child, maybe I'd be more accepted in the burrows.

But then the wolves had walked through the ridiculously short gate leading into the restaurant, and my heart had instantly longed for things it couldn't have.

Wolves were a common occurrence in the rabbit shifters' lives after the bloody battle with the coyotes. Once the fight was over, the rabbit elders met with the wolf alpha and pleaded for protection. The alpha had agreed, and over the years, the wolf pack had built their lives around us.

Rabbits were energy-filled, productive members of society, and we ran many of the town's businesses. We kept the town functioning, freeing up the wolves' time so they could focus on politics and world matters.

The arrangement worked for both species. But while we maintained a healthy respect for each other, we didn't mingle socially. Sure, rabbits eagerly helped to arrange and cater to all the werewolves' social functions, but there was a hierarchy—a.k.a. the food chain. Those on top could do what they wanted, and those on bottom let it happen.

If a wolf happened to show up at a rabbit party, no one was going to be brave enough to toss him out. We weren't forced to serve the wolves, nor were they unkind to us.

Rabbit shifters were free to go where they wished; we simply preferred to keep to ourselves outside of business. Our species didn't form bonds with each other. Not friendships, and definitely not romantic partnerships. It was unnatural.

So why did the three wolves have such an effect on me? Why did my heart flop around in my chest like a fish on land every time I saw them? Why did they keep appearing in my dreams? I huffed, blowing a loose strand of hair from my face.

In three days, it wouldn't matter.

Fingers trembling, I jabbed at the computer monitor, tapping in their breakfast order on the cracked tablet screen. That finished, I quickly checked on the diners inside the restaurant before moving toward the door that led outside. Pausing, I took a deep breath. With effort, I pasted on a smile and bounced my way onto the patio with false cheerfulness.

Chapter THREE

MONROE

My hands trembled as I refilled empty coffee mugs around the restaurant. Taking my time, I spoke with the guests at each table, all the while I fought against the invisible force trying to pull me toward the wolves' table.

When I had no other choice but to face them, I picked up their order from the kitchen and headed to their table. Unable to help myself, I drank in their features.

Syrus appeared slightly younger than Rig and Cillian, although that may have been due to his less guarded expressions. His blonde hair brushed against his broad shoulders. It wasn't the blinding yellow hue of drug store hair dye, but rather a soft golden shade that glinted in the sun. His eyes were the brown of freshly tilled soil and held an open gentleness that melted the walls I'd erected around my heart. He made me, a bunny, feel at ease, and that was no easy feat for a predator.

While Syrus seemed to have a laid-back ease, Rig seemed to be the exact opposite. His suits were always pressed with a precision that spoke of great attention to detail. Rig's cropped hair was nearly as dark as mine and reminded me of a velvet midnight sky. His hazel eyes held a keen sharpness and were tight around the corners. His face appeared fresh-shaven.

There was a part of me that hoped Rig had shaved because I'd once mentioned how he looked nice after shaving his dark stubble. The likelihood of that was slim, but it didn't stop me from dreaming. I got the distinct impression Rig wasn't the most flexible of men when it came to change, and it made me burn with a desire to ruffle his fur and see what happened when he let loose.

Finally, I drank in the vision that was Cillian. This man —er, wolf—was a green-eyed demigod if I'd ever seen one. He'd grown a beard recently, which was something I hadn't realized I liked on a guy... until now. His mahogany brown hair was shaved on both sides, but he kept it slightly longer on top, and it was always brushed to one side. He should have been in a shampoo commercial featuring hair with a ridiculous shine. Would it feel like silk sliding between my fingers?

Cillian shifted and threw an arm over the back of his seat so he could turn to watch my approach. Through his tight button-up white shirt, I could see the ripple of his muscles, and I half expected the shirt to just give up the ghost and rip. This guy must spend hours every day in a gym to stay in that shape. To my unending disappointment, the expensive fabric stretched to accommodate each of his movements. Cillian must have a fabulous tailor.

My skin heated with the weight of the three men watching me, and I took careful steps to ensure I didn't embarrass myself by tripping and falling on my face. With my heart banging around in my chest like a wild bird attempting to get free, I shifted the serving tray and began setting the food down on the table.

"You don't need to be afraid of us, Monroe." The lines around Rig's eyes softened a fraction as he spoke.

This time, it was my insides that grew warm. Hearing my name on Rig's lips was incredible. If only they knew it wasn't fear that had my pulse racing and my breath coming quicker.

It was natural they'd assume my reaction was fear; that was the typical reaction all rabbits had when they were in the presence of wolves. Heck, it was my go-to emotion whenever I knew a wolf was around. Until these three men. They were an exception.

I wasn't scared *of* them. Oh no.

I was scared of what I wanted to do *with* them.

Praying my voice wouldn't shake, I replied with a wink, "Uh-huh, sure. I've heard that's what the big bad wolf always says right before he eats you."

"I'd love to devour you," Cillian said so low that I barely caught his words. There was a thud as someone kicked him under the table, and he winced.

17

Squeaking out a nervous laugh, I finished setting the plates on the table and clutched the serving tray against my chest like a shield.

"My apologies. Normally, I have more control. I'm not sure what came over me." Cillian scratched at the back of his head while Syrus and Rig shot twin scowls at him.

"It's fine. Please don't even think about it." I smiled, knowing I was going to replay his words over and over in the privacy of my bedroom.

"Can I make up for Cillian's lack of manners by taking you to dinner?" Rig's deep voice poured over my taut nerves like warm molasses.

"I wish I could," I stammered. There was no way they could know I was about to go into heat, and spending time alone with them could only end one way—with me humping them like... well, a frickin' bunny. "But I'll be spending the next few days getting ready for the reception. And then I'll have other commitments I'll have to take care of."

The word *commitments* tasted bitter on my tongue, but that was exactly what my bonded would be. Commitments. For the past year, the elder rabbits had been hosting events every few weeks to give the unmatched females a chance to mingle with the available males.

These dinners were supposed to help make our transition into a happy little fluffle smoother after the main event. All it had done for me was prove I was still considered an outcast in our society. The females never missed an opportunity to sabotage me, and the males either ignored my presence altogether or used me as a verbal punching bag for their entertainment. I doubted I'd ever feel safe with any of the rabbit shifters.

"That's a shame." Rig looked like he wanted to say more, but the crack of a boot connecting with a shin told me someone had told him not to push the issue.

"Yeah, it is." My chin quivered; there was no hiding the pensive note in my voice.

I wanted to go to dinner with them. Just once in my life, I'd like to experience a date where the men were truly interested in me. But I didn't have that luxury. The clock was ticking, and I needed to prepare for my heat.

There was a moment of awkward silence before I shoved my feelings into the tiny little box in the back of my mind. With a forced smile, I spoke again. "Is there anything else I can do for you guys?"

"No." Syrus's smile was teasing. "Not yet, anyway."

With a choked laugh, I placed their check on the table and made my way to the back of the restaurant. It was the last time I would see these men, and the pain of that knowledge hit me like a physical blow. Only this hurt more than any punch I'd ever taken.

Chapter FOUR

MONROE

I needed to pull myself together. Instead of going inside the restaurant, I ducked behind the privacy screen we used to hide the staff break area from the patio diners. Leaning back against the cool stone wall, I took a deep, shaky breath.

Tears blurred my vision, and I closed my eyes tightly, trying to prevent them from leaking out. It was futile. Hot tears spilled from my eyes, leaving slick trails down my cheeks.

Large hands slid around my waist, and I barely managed to bite back a scream of surprise. My eyes flew open to find Cillian staring down at me.

"Hey. Don't cry." He pulled my body tight against his.

My much shorter height meant my head rested just below his pectoral muscles. I stiffened, not from fear, but from the strange intimacy of our position.

"I promise I'm not going to harm you, but I can't stand to see you upset," Cillian murmured into my hair.

I gave a soft snort and swiped at the telltale wetness on my cheeks. "I'm not afraid of you, Cillian."

"You aren't?" There was no hiding the incredulity in his tone.

Forcing myself to relax, I rested my cheek against his shirt, admiring the cloud-like soft fabric against my skin. "I've just never been held like this before. It—surprised me."

It was his turn to stiffen. "You've never been held before?"

"No—yes. Well, my parents used to hug me. But I've never been held by a guy." My voice was muffled by Cillian's shirt.

I waited, expecting him to tease me, but he remained silent. Cillian's arms tightened, and his heart thudded harder in his chest. I relished his heat and soaked in the safety I was experiencing while he held me trapped in his arms. If only this could last forever.

"Have you ever been kissed?" His voice was a hoarse whisper.

I hesitated, debating whether or not to answer. But there was something about the intimacy of the moment with him that had me answering truthfully. "Once. But the guy was drunk, and I found out later it was a dare."

A low growl rumbled in his chest, vibrating against my cheek. Why would my confession bother him? Confused and unsure what to do, I slid my arms around his waist, trying to calm him down.

We were quiet for a minute, and then Cillian rasped four words that had my body trembling. "Can I kiss you?"

I was already pushing things with the embrace. Any type of physical contact, especially this close to my first heat, could force me into an earlier heat. Worse, it could make my heat hit me even harder.

I should have said no.

But I was about to be assigned to a loveless bonding, and my only memory of a kiss was of a drunk guy and his friends shoving me around. I wanted a memory I could tuck away in my mind. A memory I could pull out when I needed to remember what it was like to be kissed by someone I felt a connection with.

Pulling my cheek away from his shirt, I tilted my head up to look at him. "Yes."

Cillian needed no further encouragement. His hand caught my chin, and he leaned down. Standing on my tiptoes, I met him partway. Our lips touched, and the world tilted and faded away, until only Cillian and I were left on the entire planet.

His lips were gentle, tasting and exploring my lips. I tried to hold still, needing to etch this memory into my brain to last the rest of my life. When the tip of his tongue slid along my lower lip, I couldn't help it. My lips parted a fraction, and I moaned.

Cillian took advantage of the opening and plunged his tongue inside my mouth. His tongue was like velvet, teasing and stroking along my tongue. It was the biggest turn-on I'd ever experienced. My knees buckled, and I grasped at his shirt to stay upright.

"Started without us? That's dirty even for you, Cillian." Rig's low voice came from behind me, and a delicious shiver tickled my spine.

Rig's hands rested on my waist, and then he lifted me up. Not loving the feeling of my feet being off the ground, I threw my arms around Cillian's neck and wrapped my legs around his waist, not caring when it caused my ruffled skirt to ride up my thighs.

Rig pressed in tight against my back, sandwiching me between the two wolves. If I'd possessed a single shred of rabbit shifter survival instinct, I should've been quaking in my tennis shoes. Instead of running, I tightened my legs around Cillian's waist and whimpered into his mouth.

I guess my bullies had been right after all. I was a defective bunny.

"Do you know how badly I've wanted to touch you?" Rig whispered in my ear. His hands slid along my thighs, and the brush of his fingers on my exposed skin caused me to ache for his touch in other places.

Cillian continued his passionate assault on my mouth, making it impossible to respond to Rig, although I doubted I could've strung two coherent words together, anyway.

"This is ridiculously unfair." Syrus's whine came from a million miles away. "If your boss wasn't looking for you, I'd be kneeling beneath you to kiss your other set of lips."

My brain short-circuited at the visual image his words

conjured up. Sweat beaded across my already scorching skin. Finally, I caught up with the first part of what Syrus had said.

My boss was looking for me.

It was only a matter of time before he checked back here; it wasn't like there were a whole lot of places an employee could hide in such a tiny restaurant. If my boss found me in a compromising position, word would spread fast through the burrows. That was the absolute last thing I wanted to deal with, mere days before I would go through my first heat.

Breaking the kiss, I wiggled and shoved hard against Cillian's chest. "My boss can't find me like this. Let me down!" My voice was shrill with panic, and my heart fluttered faster than a hummingbird's wings.

"Whoa. Calm down," Syrus whispered. "I told him I thought I'd seen you out front, and he headed that way."

"Good!" Rig purred, spinning me around so I was facing him. His lips were against my mouth in an instant. The kiss was full of rough demands and sinful promises. My toes curled in my shoes, and when he put me back on my feet, I staggered, trying to find my equilibrium.

"I—uh." I tried to find the words for what I wanted to tell them, but I didn't even know what that was. Should I tell them goodbye? Thank them for giving me a moment of passion I could savor for the rest of my life?

In the end, I said nothing. I straightened my skirt and brushed back the hair that had tumbled free of my braid. Eyes down, I moved back toward the patio. I paused beside

Syrus, and before I could change my mind, I went up on my tiptoes and kissed him. The kiss was sweet, and far more PG than the kisses I'd just shared with the other two wolves, but it was incredible in a different way.

Hearing my boss calling my name, I quickly backed away from him and rushed toward the patio. It took every ounce of willpower I possessed not to look back over my shoulder. In a perfect world, I'd have wanted those men to be my bonded. But the world was far from perfect, and it had shattered my dreams and hopes long ago.

My heart may belong to the three sexy wolves, but my body never could... not if I hoped to bring honor to my parents' memory by taking my place in the burrows.

Chapter FIVE

RIG

I yanked off my work clothes and tossed them onto a nearby chair. Turning to the dresser, I pulled open a drawer with far too much force. The drawer hurtled off its roller track and crashed to the floor, where the contents emptied onto the thick white carpet.

Cursing under my breath, I quickly cleaned up the mess my agitation had caused. That was pretty much all I'd done all day—clean up messes caused by yours truly. It'd been three days since the kiss with Monroe, and she hadn't been back to work. Her boss wasn't giving us any information about when she might return, either.

With each passing day, my mood became more unstable. I was like an addict craving my next fix—of her. My wolf wasn't faring much better and had spent the day pacing non-stop inside my mind. I was physically and mentally exhausted, but I knew if I tried to sleep now, my mind

would just fixate on the one thing I couldn't have...
Monroe.

Slipping into my soft gray sweats, I reached into another drawer for a black tee, trying to ignore the way my hand shook. I was going to have to talk to Cillian at some point; he was the alpha, after all. Even if my wolf had picked Monroe as my lifemate, she shouldn't be affecting me so much.

Physical contact, like the touching and our brief kiss, would begin to build a mate bond, but it shouldn't have escalated this quickly. Last time we'd talked, Cillian hadn't even been sure how strong of a bond could be formed between bunny shifters and wolf shifters.

The soft rap of knuckles against the door frame caused me to jerk. I hadn't heard anyone coming. That wasn't a good thing for a wolf, especially when I could usually hear houseflies humping in the house next door.

Cillian leaned against the door. "Brett has invited us to visit the pack house to eat pizza and watch TV with some of the guys. I know you would prefer to stay in, but it has been a while since we socialized with the pack. Syrus and I are going to leave in five minutes. It's your decision if you want to come, but I'd appreciate your presence."

It was a request, not an order. Cillian wouldn't be angry if I declined, but looking at the lines of fatigue around his eyes, I knew I would go. Even though he was exhausted, Cillian still had to show up and be the supportive pack alpha his men looked up to. Syrus and I were Cillian's support system, so it was a given that we would go with him.

Sighing, I nodded. "I'll come with you. Just give me a minute to grab my shoes, and I'll meet you downstairs."

"Thanks, Rig." Cillian turned to leave but then paused, looking at me over his shoulder. "We'll find her. I've already put a call in to my contact at the burrows."

I watched him leave, feeling slightly better. The rabbit elders wouldn't risk upsetting the wolf alpha. If Cillian asked a favor, they were likely going to be eager to help.

WE ARRIVED at the pack house thirty minutes later. Grabbing a slice of pizza, I began working my way through the guys gathered there. The pack had grown by leaps and bounds over the past decade under Cillian's leadership.

"Hey! Everyone needs to get in here! It's starting!" Brett called from the theater room. His announcement was answered with loud whoops and shrill catcalls.

"What's starting?" I asked the guy who was handing out cold sodas.

"The Bunny Bang Bash!" he answered with a laugh. At my look of confusion, he continued. "You know? The Rabbit Reception?"

I didn't keep up with what the rabbit shifters did in their free time, nor did I spend time watching TV, so I still didn't have a clue what he was talking about. "Never heard of it. Why is everyone so excited about watching a rabbit party?"

Brett stepped up behind me and slapped me on the back. "Rig, man! You need to get out more! It's only the second time the rabbits have televised the event. It's better than any reality TV show humans have thought up. Basically, in the spring, the old rabbits parade the smoking-hot female bunnies through a crowd of potential mates. The girls are about to go into heat, and everyone is hyped on hormones. Last year, some of the bunnies started getting hot and heavy as soon as they were matched. It was sexy as frick, man."

My stomach churned, and I tossed the last of my pizza into a nearby trash can. Undeterred, Brett pushed me toward the movie room, and my limbs moved reflexively. My eyes locked onto the wall-sized television screen, and I was unable to look away. This was stupid.

The likelihood of Monroe being there was slim, right?

The event was already in full swing, and I watched the girls in elegant silk gowns of various colors move out onto the floor.

"Each table is a family group of male rabbits. The girls have been matched by the elders to their male group. See the crystal bunny in the center of each table?" Brett sipped his drink as he explained what we were watching.

"The ice sculpture-looking thing?" My vocal cords had grown stiff, causing my voice to come out gruff.

"Exactly. This part is pretty cool. Every girl is wearing a bracelet that has been paired with one of the crystals on the tables. They'll walk around the tables, and when they get near the table they've been paired with, the crystal and bracelet will glow."

He continued rambling about the gossip surrounding the matches and wondering out loud whether it was random or if the elders took bribes, but I'd stopped listening. The camera had zoomed in on the procession of girls, and there in the back stood Monroe.

My Monroe.

Cold sweat broke out on my body, and my stomach plummeted toward the floor.

Unlike the bright yellows, greens, blues, and every shade of red on the blanket, Monroe wore a dove gray gown. It was a simple dress, lacking the delicate beadwork and yards of fabric trains that the other gowns had. The dress should have appeared cheap by comparison. Instead, it made her look like a ruling queen among fluttering princesses.

"Easy, Rig." Cillian's voice was low as he stepped beside me and took the mangled soda can from my hand.

Anger boiled inside me. Why hadn't she told us? She'd toyed with us that last day in the café, letting us think she was interested, all the while knowing she was days away from basically being married.

"Did you know?" The words were barely intelligible through my clenched teeth.

"I'd heard of this event, but hadn't ever looked into it. Until Monroe, I had no reason to care about bunny social behaviors." Cillian's tone was flat, but I'd known him long enough to know that it was his go-to for covering emotion.

"She's scared." Syrus's shoulder bumped against mine as he moved to stand next to me. "Monroe doesn't want to be there."

Squinting at the TV, I waited for the camera to pan toward her again. When it did, I studied her features as she followed behind the rest of the laughing girls. A stiff smile was frozen on her beautiful face. She wore only light makeup, and it didn't cover the red skin around her eyes. Monroe had been crying.

If this was supposed to be the happiest day of her life, then something had gone horribly wrong. Why did Monroe look like she was walking to her execution rather than about to meet her beloved bonded? I didn't have to wait long to get my answers.

Chapter SIX

MONROE

The girls around me were all smiles as they twirled their way between the tables, dancing to music I was unable to hear over the pounding of my heart in my ears. We were playing a life-changing game of Hot and Cold, where our future mates were the hidden object we were supposed to find.

Lights glittered overhead, catching on the opulent table place settings, and sparkling off the expensive beadwork that adorned every gown in the room. Well, every gown except mine. I loved the simplicity of my dress, but while we'd waited backstage, the rest of the girls hadn't been shy about voicing their feelings about it being 'boring.'

Brushing my fingers across the silky fabric, I smiled. It was the most beautiful thing I'd ever owned, and I'd paid for it with the tips I'd saved from waitressing at the café. The elders were supposed to pay for every girl to get a custom gown designed and sewn for them, but I hadn't been surprised when none of the dressmakers in the burrows had availability for me.

It seemed every girl in the burrow needed a full wardrobe for their bonding week, and I'd lacked the piles of cash needed to bribe my way to the front of the seamstresses' schedules. Excluding a female who was being matched shouldn't have been allowed, but my emails to the event organizers regarding my need for a suitable bonding gown had gone unanswered. Just like every other email I'd ever sent them.

If I'd been wealthy, my treatment would have been different. Since being protected by the wolves, the rabbit shifters had flourished. Deals were created, and businesses were launched. Wealth and prestige became things that suddenly mattered in the burrows. The rabbit men who were invited to sit in meetings with the wolves gained respect among our kind.

As an orphan and the sole survivor of my family line, I lacked both wealth and political standing among the rabbits. The only thing I had of value was my body. A healthy female rabbit, even a poor one, was considered a treasure by the elders. Not for our brilliant brains, but because of our baby-producing ability.

"All that glitters is not gold," I murmured under my breath.

It didn't matter how beautifully they adorned the room and the women in it; all this night was about was matching a womb with the men desperate to fill it. The elders and most of the men in the room viewed the unmatched females as little more than breeders. And as much as I despised it, I'd still shown up tonight and allowed them to tie the crystal bracelet to my wrist.

My stomach twisted, and I pressed my hand against it, willing it to settle. What choice did I have? I had nowhere else to go. A rabbit alone in the world could never survive. We were prey, not predators. Our strength came from numbers.

If I ever hoped to honor my family line and find acceptance in the burrows, this was my one and only shot. With that ringing in my head, I walked near each table, carefully avoiding eye contact. I focused on watching for the telltale glowing of the rabbit crystal that would signify I'd found my lifemates. My bonded.

Every couple of minutes, the crowd would cheer, and I'd hear girlish squeals as matches were made. Sweat slid down my spine, and I fought to keep my breathing even. Part of me was anxious I wouldn't find my match, but part of me was equally terrified I would.

The only men I'd ever wanted weren't here, not that a pairing between us would have worked, anyway. I was on the lowest rung of society in the burrows, which meant I was miles below the wolves.

The bracelet on my wrist flickered, the light warm against my skin. I was getting closer. My steps slowed as I forced myself to put one foot in front of the other. The crystal on the table in front of me glowed a flowery purple, the same shade of pale purple as the bracelet on my wrist.

Pulling my gaze from the crystal, I looked at the men seated around the table. The world around me tilted, and black ink filled my vision as I fought desperately not to pass out. Wrapping my arms around my waist, I pinched myself, praying this was a nightmare, and I'd wake up any minute.

But I didn't wake up, and this wasn't a dream. My lip trembled when I realized that this was very much happening.

The five faces staring back at me held expressions ranging from disgust to shock to malicious glee. These men were the elders' sons. They might as well have been rabbit royalty for how everyone adored them, which is why their treatment of me had always been overlooked, excused, or completely ignored.

These were the men who were likely to run the burrows one day, and every single girl here tonight had wanted them. Except me. I'd hoped for anyone but them.

"Unbelievable." Zane threw up his hands.

"Be nice, Zane. Aren't you going to come greet us, loner?" Seth taunted me. His lips would have been beautiful if not twisted in a perpetual sneer when he looked at me. He'd told Zane to be nice, but instead of easing my anxiety, it caused my worry to shoot through the roof.

"Yeah, you wouldn't want to embarrass yourself by running like a scared little bunny, would you?" Malcolm coaxed, something dark glinting in his eyes.

Seth pushed his chair back from the table, spreading his legs and opening his arms. "Come here. Be a good girl."

I hesitated, my eyes darting around the room. What was

36

I searching for? Help? An escape? Neither option presented itself. Half the room was busy making out, while the rest stood open-mouthed, not bothering to hide their stares as they watched the burrow's golden boys... and me.

Were the spectators expecting me to reject the match? Or maybe they were waiting for the men to reject me? A rejection had never happened in our history, and as much as I despised these guys, I'd never disrespect the elders' decision by walking away from their decision. Not to mention, my body couldn't survive the heat alone. This was all that I had.

Straightening my wobbling spine and pushing back my shoulders, I made my way to Seth.

"That's a good little bun," he purred, causing my skin to prickle in fear.

I tried to sit in the seat next to him, but with a laugh, Seth wrapped his arm around my waist, shoved my flowing skirt up to my knees, and pulled me onto his lap so that I straddled him. "Oh!" was all I managed to say before his lips slammed against mine.

Chapter SEVEN

MONROE

I tried to pull away, but his fingers sank into my hair, pinning me in place. His kiss became crushing, and he pushed for me to open my mouth and give his tongue entrance. I resisted, only to feel his teeth sink into my bottom lip.

Seth likely wanted to incite my heat by teasing me with pleasure and pain, but instead of stirring needy feelings within me, my mind focused on the bitter, coppery taste of blood filling my mouth.

This kiss was far different from the gentle, passionate kisses I'd experienced with the wolves. They'd given as much as they'd taken, taking cues from how I'd responded to them. Seth was only interested in what he could take.

Chairs scraped the floor as the other guys scooted closer to Seth's seat. Someone's hands slid up my hips and waist, while lips pressed to the back of my neck. From the corner of my eye, I could see Tom and Jordy waiting for their turn. Either that or they had a thing for watching. Disgust swirled in my gut.

I should've been over the moon with the attention of these men, especially with my first heat mere hours away. For the past several hours, the heat's build-up had been bubbling beneath the surface of my skin. This was the point of the entire event. Match up horny rabbits who would procreate in order to expand our species.

Then why did all of this feel so wrong? Instead of it feeling natural, or like the rite of passage it was supposed to be, it made me feel dirty and… used.

Zane's hand grasped my chin, jerking my head toward him. My jaw popped under the pressure of his grip. "Do you know how much I've wanted your body?"

I wanted to ask him if that was before or after he'd knocked me around the high school and burrow meeting hall. And what about all the other times he'd humiliated me? But if we were going to turn over a new leaf tonight, then I wasn't going to bring up the past. Pushing past the memories, I shook my head.

"Don't worry. Tonight, I will show you." Zane pulled my mouth to his, kissing me with a force that would no doubt leave bruises on my pale skin.

Warning bells clanged in my mind. I'd been taught that a heat could be rough on a female, but her bonded males were supposed to be gentle and make her feel safe. This was all wrong.

Still, I hesitated. What if there was something wrong

with me? My body should be flooded with hormones, and I should be trying to rip Seth's clothes off. Maybe I was defective. An icy shiver slid down my spine, not of delight, but disgust. I was trying to accept this situation and be the good little rabbit I was supposed to be, but the urge to flee was building to a crescendo inside me.

Seth's hands grabbed my hips, grinding me down against his hard erection. He groaned, and his nostrils flared with desire. I tried to imagine it was Cillian's hands on my body, willing to try anything to make this situation more bearable. It didn't help. In fact, it made Seth's touch even more repulsive, and my mind recoiled.

Bile rose in my throat at the vulgarness of Seth's movements, but deep inside, a tiny flame flickered to life. My heat. It didn't matter if I wanted nothing to do with these men. My rabbit's nature only cared that there were willing males in the vicinity, and I felt the heat bubble closer to the surface. I was being betrayed by my body's instincts.

Tears clung to my eyelashes. I would be helpless to stop the heat once it fully took over. Until the heat subsided, I would be at the mercy of the men mating me. But how could I trust these men to protect and care for me?

Malcolm slipped a finger under one of my gown's delicate straps. With a quick rip, it snapped, and my dress started to slide down over my chest. I quickly snatched the fabric and clutched it against my chest. Seth pulled back, a small smile on his face. He sent a knowing look to Malcolm. With one sharp movement, Seth shoved to his feet, toppling me onto the floor.

Crying out in shock, I grasped at my torn gown while the rest of the guys laughed down at me. Seth cleared his throat and addressed the elders who sat on the stage overseeing their matches like pompous kings surveying their kingdom.

"Esteemed elders," Seth began, his deep baritone voice filled with cocky arrogance. "I believe a mistake has been made today. While Monroe is a sweet girl, she just isn't cut out to be the mother of the next generation of our burrow's leaders. My family and I ask that you please accept our request to attend next spring's reception to find a suitable female to stand by our side."

My brain struggled to understand what was going on, and when it did, panic surged inside me, a tsunami prepared to destroy what was left of my broken soul. This couldn't be happening. The room had grown eerily silent, everyone holding their breaths.

"But what am I supposed to do?" I asked, my words a broken whisper.

Seth paused, glancing down at me. His expression was caring, almost thoughtful, but his eyes were cold. He arranged his lips into a sad, sympatric smile and faced the elders again.

"We understand that this represents a problem for Monroe. With her upcoming heat so close, it would be impossible to find her assistance at such short notice. Therefore, we are willing to take the time from our schedules to see her through her heat as well as her future heats. We will provide a home and food for her so that she isn't a burden on the burrow's resources. We just will not be producing heirs with her."

Seth's words were more effective than a punch to my stomach. I wasn't even suitable to reproduce with? There was no way the elders would agree to this, would they? I couldn't breathe as I waited for them to speak up and defend me.

The elders conferred with each other for less than a minute before they clambered to their feet. They'd reached a decision quickly... far too quickly. "This is highly unusual. As elders, we take great pride in creating the best matches for future offspring. However, we have discussed your request, and in honor of your many contributions to the burrows, we agree to allow you to attend the ball again next spring and find a match you feel is more suitable."

The elderly, gray-haired man who I'd once thought kind turned his cloudy blue eyes on me. "You are a lucky girl to have these energetic young men willing to care for you. This is such an honor for you, Monroe."

"An honor?" I choked out.

They were sentencing me to a life without love, without respect, and without a chance to produce children to honor my family line. I'd always be an outcast. Worse, I'd be a toy for these men to use as they saw fit, and the elders would ignore any mistreatment their golden boys dished out on me.

Zane reached down, gently pulling me to my feet. Pressing his lips to my ear, he whispered, "And just like that, you belong to us. Our little whore."

It was that last word and his groping hands that finally propelled my frozen body into action. My knee found the erection straining against Zane's pants with a satisfyingly hard thud, and he tumbled to the ground in pain.

I didn't wait to see what would happen next. Giving into my terror, I took off like the scared rabbit I was. I didn't care what predators awaited me in a life outside the burrows... None could be worse than those in this room.

Chapter EIGHT

CILLIAN

I stared at the TV, emotions roiling in me like a volcano preparing to erupt.

My heart stopped beating when I spotted Monroe's sweet face and realized she was about to be snatched from my life forever.

"Why didn't she tell us or give us a chance?" Syrus's voice was hoarse, and he gave a quick swipe at the corner of his eye.

Syrus was soft for a wolf, but no one in the pack dared to tease him over it. Not when his best friends were the alpha and the beta. Not to mention, he could hold his own in a fight.

"Because we were nothing more than nice strangers. We weren't direct enough." Rig's voice was flat, his eyes glassy dark orbs.

"It was more likely because we are wolves. Rabbits mate

rabbits, wolves mate wolves," I added, the words bitter on my tongue.

It didn't have to be that way, but the age-old survival instincts between predator and prey, along with old shifter traditions, made it seem like an impossibility for Monroe to be with us.

Rig cursed when Monroe's bracelet began to glow, matching her with a table of male rabbits. Disgust knocked the wind from my lungs when I recognized them from the business meetings I'd held with the burrows. The TV crew loved the guys, though, because they ignored all the other tables and guests. Instead, they kept the cameras zoomed in on Monroe as the male rabbits put their hands—and lips— all over her.

The wolves scattered around the room whistled and cheered, taking bets on how far things would go while the show was still being recorded live. I wanted to scream at them to shut up, but my vocal cords were frozen.

In my mind, I could still feel Monroe's soft curves pressed against my body, and it made watching these men with her even more distasteful. We'd been nothing more than a warm-up for her. My wolf's howl of pain echoed around my skull.

"Monroe's upset." Syrus leaned forward and squinted at the TV screen.

"You're wrong. She seemed pretty eager to jump in Seth's lap." Rig snarled.

"No! Look closer!" Syrus's words vibrated with urgency.

"Her body is as stiff as a board. She isn't relaxing into their touch like she did with you and Cillian."

The last thing on earth I wanted to do was to look closer as the rabbit men ravished the only person my wolf had ever wanted. In the end, curiosity got the better of me, and I found myself taking a halting step toward the TV. The camera zoomed in tight on Seth and Monroe's faces.

What. The. Frick. Syrus was right.

Seth's face was a mask of raw desire—and something else I couldn't put my finger on. But Monroe's face was void of all emotion. Even when being kissed, she never kissed the guy back, and her eyes stayed open.

When she'd been in my arms, her beautiful thick eyelashes had dropped. She had given me the sexy bunny come-hither bedroom eyes. While I kissed her, Monroe's cheeks had flushed a rosy pink, and her body had melted against me. She'd clung to my shirt, using the grip to pull me closer and keep herself steady.

Monroe had been just as turned on by my touch as I had been by hers.

Looking at her now, I saw none of those things. Every time a man at that table touched Monroe's body, her muscles would tighten, and she seemed to fight the desire to shy away.

"Why doesn't she just tell them no?" Syrus ran his hand through his hair, his jaw ticking in frustration.

"Um. Am I missing something? Why does it matter so much to you?" Brett's eyes darted between Syrus's face and the TV. "Wait a second. That's the waitress at that café you guys love so much, isn't it?"

"Drop it," I ordered, pushing an alpha command into the two words. I'd answer his questions later. Right then, my entire focus was on the scene playing out on the screen in front of me.

My confusion and heartache were quickly followed by a fury hotter than all the fires of Hades as I watched the men rip Monroe's dress strap. They nearly exposed her breasts to the entire room, and everyone watching the drama from their homes.

Seth stood suddenly, letting Monroe's delicate body slam against the concrete floor like she was nothing more than a dirty napkin.

The wolves in the room growled and shouted their disapproval over Monroe's rough treatment. It didn't matter if they knew her or not; that type of cruelty wasn't tolerated. If a wolf had dared to treat his mate that way, he'd find it difficult to walk for weeks, even with our accelerated healing abilities.

Syrus staggered to an empty chair and collapsed into it, his face turning a pale green.

"I'm going to kill him." Rig's facial features hadn't changed, and his voice was flat, making his threat all the more terrifying.

I'd known Rig since we were both pups. He always followed through. Seth was a dead man walking.

My eyes shot back to the TV. Seth was speaking, and I wanted to know what he was saying. "SILENCE!"

48

Deafening silence fell on the room after my roared order.

In the end, I wish I hadn't known what he spoke to the elders or how the elders had accepted their request as though they'd been doing Monroe a great kindness. She wasn't a burden. No, she was a blessing, yet they were treating her as though she was an unwanted pet needing a home. I'd always seen the rabbits as gentle, sweet creatures who needed protection. Now I saw their true colors, and horror sank into my bones.

These rabbits were vicious creatures, capable of unbelievable cruelty toward their own.

I would never forget this.

A growl ripped from my throat as Zane reached down and lifted Monroe to her feet. He whispered something to her that the microphones didn't pick up.

"Syrus!" I barked. He'd learned to read lips one summer when he was a bored teenager, and it had proven to be a surprisingly handy ability.

When he finally spoke, Syrus's voice was mechanical, and he croaked out the vile words. "And just like that, you belong to us. Our little whore."

The room erupted into chaos. Wolves pelted the wall and television with bottles and cans, their outraged growls shaking the room. If I'd wanted to, I could have ordered them to take out Seth and his friends, and the pack would have shifted and carried out my command with glee. But the command caught in my throat when Monroe clutched her tattered dress against her chest and raced out of view.

No, I wouldn't give the order.

Because I wanted to kill them myself.

They would regret the day they dared to touch Monroe. *My Monroe.*

My clothes turned to shreds as I released my wolf, allowing the shift to ripple over my body.

I thundered through the pack house with Syrus and Rig hot on my heels. Outside, I lifted my snout to the midnight black sky and howled a bloodcurdling warning... one of a predator on the hunt for its prey.

Tonight, after finding my precious Monroe, I had plans to keep the Grim Reaper busy.

Chapter NINE

CILLIAN

T he hard thud of my paws in the dirt matched the pounding beat of my heart.

Where are we going? Syrus's voice drifted through my mind.

To eat some rabbit, Rig snapped.

I was losing control of my wolf, and my human consciousness began to fade as my wolf pushed to the forefront. With immense effort, I fought to maintain a semblance of my humanity because, without it, I knew exactly how this night would go down. It would be far worse than the night the coyotes attacked the burrows.

The rabbits have grown fat and self-centered under our protection. They brought this on their own heads, Rig snarled.

Rig wasn't wrong. The rabbits would pay for their treatment of Monroe. My Monroe. But first, we needed to find her. She was our priority.

Where do you think she is? Syrus, always the level-headed one between us, asked.

I think she'd want to get as far away from them as possible, I responded, lifting my nose into the air and hoping to catch her scent.

But what makes you think she would run in this direction? Rig asked. *She might have run to the opposite side of the burrows.*

I hesitated before answering. *I'm hoping she ran toward us.*

Rig snorted. *She's a bunny... our prey. You think she would willingly run to wolves while terrified?*

I growled at his disrespectful tone, forcefully reminding him who was alpha. *Yes. Tonight, the rabbits proved themselves to be vicious. But who better to protect her than a predator every shifter on earth feared?*

I prayed my logic was accurate—that maybe, just maybe, some small part of her subconscious knew we would be her shield.

But we needed to find Monroe before any other shifter did.

Plus, Monroe likes us, Syrus added with a calm certainty I envied.

Falling silent other than our raspy breathing, we covered mile after mile of thick woods and underbrush. When I caught the sweet scent of jasmine blossoms drifting in the wind, my wolf released a victorious howl.

We'd caught her scent. Now it was just a matter of time before we found our girl.

Syrus and Rig's howls blended with mine. It was a bone-chilling harmony. A warning to those who crossed us and a reassuring promise to the one who needed us.

I licked my long canines, relishing the thought of ripping into Seth's body. I wanted to watch his vile blood drain into the soil. My muscles tightened, and bloodlust consumed me until my vision was tinted crimson.

Focus, Cil. There will be time for vengeance later, Syrus urged.

The tantalizing scent of jasmine grew stronger. Straining my ears, I picked up the faint but steady thump-thump of a heartbeat. *We're close. Less than two miles away.*

With a burst of adrenaline, I sped across the leaf-covered forest floor with Syrus and Rig on either side of my wolf. Leaping over a massive fallen log, I skidded to a stop in a tiny clearing. She was here, but where?

Thump-thump-thump.

My gaze darted around the forest, my enhanced eyesight making it as bright as if lit by the sun.

In the log, Rig whispered, as though worried she might hear our thoughts and run.

The log? It was large, but was it large enough for a human? I moved closer to the log. Reaching one end, I laid down on my belly and peered into the hollowed-out trunk of the ancient oak tree.

She was there. Moonlight caught on the fabric of her dress, causing it to glow. Her hair had fallen from the elegant style she'd pinned it up in for the rabbit reception, and it cascaded around her face.

53

Her large luminous eyes watched me, but she made no effort to scoot away from me. My wolf was pleased, although I reminded him that Monroe had no way of knowing who we were while in our shifted form.

Whining softly, I dropped my snout onto my massive paws, hoping to convey I wasn't a threat to her. Rig and Syrus moved to either side of me and did the same. For several long minutes, we lay there, breathing in the calming scent of moss... and Monroe. She'd always smelled incredible, but tonight it was alluring and absolutely edible. My mouth watered even as I wondered what had caused her scent to change.

Monroe's muscles slowly relaxed, and she rested her tear-streaked cheek on her palm while she studied us. Her gray silk gown was ripped and splotched with dark stains. There was a faint scent of blood hanging in the air, and I hoped it was from the sharp thistles covering the forest floor.

There would be no place on earth for the rabbits to hide if they'd shed so much as a drop of her blood.

Monroe's lips parted, and she broke the silence. "You're Cillian."

It wasn't a question, but rather a statement. Lifting my head, I gave an awkward nod.

A small, heartbreaking smile teased the corner of her mouth. Wincing, she pushed herself up onto her hands and knees. Keeping one hand on the top of her dress, she carefully shimmied her way out of the log. Reaching us, she threw her arms around my wolf's neck without hesitation and burst into tears.

Unable to speak but wanting to comfort her, I licked her bare shoulder and whined. Monroe's arms tightened as she clung to me, soaking my fur with her salty tears.

"I was trying to fi-find my way to you, but got confused and scared." Monroe's body shook with racking sobs. "But I kne-knew you'd find me. Th-that all three of you would come for me."

I wanted to shift so I could hold her in my arms, but my wolf refused to relinquish control of our form. At the light touch of her fingers stroking my coat, I stopped struggling against my wolf. If petting me helped to calm her, then I would happily sign up to be her emotional support wolf.

To my unending embarrassment, my tail smacked the ground, tossing leaves and dirt into the air around us. Rig and Syrus huffed a laugh, completely ignoring the narrow-eyed glare I shot in their direction. I couldn't help my joy. Monroe had known we would come for her and waited for us. It was another step toward getting her to trust us.

Not wanting to be left out, Syrus and Rig crawled toward her on their bellies. They kept their movements slow, being careful not to startle her. She hadn't grown up in a pack, so she couldn't possibly understand how big of a deal this was. None of us had ever reduced ourselves to such demeaning positions for anyone—not even each other. But for Monroe, *our Monroe*, we would do anything to make sure she felt safe.

Curling their massive white wolves around her body,

my pack mates made sure Monroe was tucked safely between the three of us. Monroe stroked both wolves in turn, and ever so slowly, her tears began to subside. Her eyelids drooped, and her body sank against me as exhaustion finally overwhelmed her.

I knew she wouldn't be able to hear me, but I couldn't keep from whispering to her in my mind. *Rest, beautiful. No one will dare touch you.*

Chapter TEN

S Y R U S

Monroe's breathing gradually slowed and evened out. Her eyes fluttered closed, sending a wave of awe washing through me.

She's sleeping? I asked through the bond.

Yes. This shouldn't be possible, especially so soon, Cillian responded.

Monroe trusted us enough to fall asleep while surrounded by three wolves. It was a huge statement of how she already felt toward us. Or maybe it was just a sign of how exhausted she was after the night's mayhem. A fresh surge of anger shot through me. Monroe should never have gone through the humiliation the rabbits had dished out at their party.

We lay there for another two hours, protecting Monroe as she slept. None of us wanted to disturb her sleep. The night was calm, and everything was going fine… right up until the air began to hum around her.

The clean scent of ozone wafted around us, causing my nose to twitch. *What is goin —*

My question was cut off when Monroe's shift rippled across her body. It turned our sleeping beauty into a sleeping bunny. How she managed to sleep through a shift was beyond me, but my heart melted at the tiny dove gray rabbit nestled inside the silk gown. It was the cutest thing I'd ever seen.

Awwww. Cillian, Rig, and I drawled at the same time in the mental link.

It was also the first time I'd seen a rabbit shifter perform their shift. Rabbits preferred to remain in their much larger human forms when around wolves. I couldn't blame them. If I was the natural prey of a particular predator, I'd avoid shifting and tempting them with my delicious self, too.

I nuzzled the tiny furball. Her back legs twitched, but she continued sleeping soundly. Even her bunny form trusted us, and that knowledge had a warmth blossoming in my chest.

If I'd felt protective of her before, it was nothing compared to how I felt now. Monroe was in her weakest form, and I would destroy anyone who so much as looked at her twice.

Now what? We should probably get her back home before dawn. I hesitated, hating the idea of waking her, but my wolf refused to relax with her tiny shifter form at risk from, well, everything.

We should, Cillian's wolf huffed. He lumbered to his feet, careful to avoid jostling Monroe's tiny bunny body. It reminded me of the memes posted online where people refused to get up because their cat was sleeping on their lap, and they didn't want to disturb them.

Rig and I rose to our paws, and all three of us stared down at the sleeping puff of fluff. If anyone had stumbled upon us in the woods at that precise moment, it would've looked like we were planning our next meal.

Who's going to wake her? Rig asked while taking a step back. Clearly, he didn't plan to do it.

An idea tumbled through my mind. *Wait a sec! Let me try something.*

Taking a step forward, I gathered the top and bottom of her gown in my massive jaws. It took a couple of tries, but I managed to create a hammock with our sleeping bunny curled up inside. She released a contented squeak, and I smiled, almost dropping the fabric.

Idiot. Keep your mouth shut while carrying her. Got it? Rig snarled.

You're just jealous you didn't think of it, and now I get to carry her home, I taunted him over my shoulder as I turned and pranced my way toward our house.

Rig gave a low growl behind me, then he and Cillian moved to flank me, providing protection. Although I doubted we'd need it. Cillian was an alpha in peak condition, and there wasn't a creature in these woods stupid enough to challenge him.

Blessedly, the trip home was uneventful. The pastel hues

of sunrise had begun to paint the sky when we finally climbed the front porch steps of our home. Cillian quickly shifted and pressed the passcode into the keypad that would unlock the front door. This was the best invention ever since wolves lacked pockets to carry keys in. Rig and I followed Cillian into the house.

Rig shifted and caught a white robe that Cillian tossed his way. Unwilling to put my precious bundle down, I remained in my wolf form and eyed them.

"Let's take her up to the main bedroom and settle her into bed." Cillian rubbed the back of his neck. For the first time since I'd known him, he looked worried.

"Are you sure we shouldn't put her in a guest room? At least until we've had time to talk to her?" Rig asked, and just like Cillian, he sounded uncertain.

I knew why they were hesitating.

The main bedroom had never been used. We'd spent years preparing the room for our future mate. It was the room we would share with the female we claimed as our own. A room just for her and where no other female had ever stepped foot. We'd prepared every little detail with our dream mate in mind.

Countless hours had been spent making sure it was perfect—from the throw pillows on the massive bed to the feminine products in the medicine cabinet in the bathroom.

If we took a female in there who ended up deciding she didn't want to be our mate... well, then the entire room would need to be dismantled. Or maybe we would burn the house to the ground and start again.

Our eyes locked, each of us weighing our feelings for the gray bunny balled up in the silk sling I carried. I knew my answer, and I watched their expressions as they came to the same conclusion. She was our mate. We just needed to convince her that she wanted to claim us as well.

Cillian reached out to take the sling from my mouth but stopped at my low whine. Turning, I made my way toward the stairs. I lifted my head to avoid bumping her body against the polished wood steps. My progress was slow, but it was worth the extra effort when she didn't wake.

Rig moved ahead of me down the hallway and opened the bedroom door. Elation and fear churned in my stomach. I'd dreamed of this day for what felt like forever. But I'd always imagined we'd lead our beautiful mate into this room. And that was nothing like the current reality.

My nails clicked against the painted wood floor as I padded into the room. We'd painted the wood a soft turquoise, and then sanded the new paint down, giving the boards an aged patina appearance. I'd never admit to the embarrassing amount of time we'd spent reading magazines and home decor blogs to figure out what our woman might like. Then we'd spent hours recreating those things in our future bride's room. The floor had been one of those things.

I moved to the center of the room and stopped. The bed was unusual by both wolf and human standards. Instead of a typical four-poster bed, we'd created a dropped floor in the center of the room. It was like a pit, so instead of climbing up into a bed, we'd crawl down into it. The bed had a custom mattress that was ten feet by ten feet. A down-filled comforter covered the mattress while piles of colorful blankets and pillows lined the edges.

Pausing, I looked at the other two men. *I think I should stay in my wolf form. She fell asleep in the forest, surrounded by the white fur of our wolves. Waking up in a house with three men might be traumatic after the crap she went through tonight.*

That's smart. Cillian tapped a finger against his temple. *Perhaps we should all change back?*

I considered his words, then slowly shook my head. *She is going to want to talk when she wakes up. If we are all in wolf form, then we'd need to shift back. Monroe might not appreciate the eye-full of naked men as soon as she wakes up. Speaking of which, you two should put some pants on.*

Easing down the steps and onto the mattress, I made my way toward the center of the bed. I lowered the silk dress down and let the fabric fall open, revealing our beautiful mate.

She'd managed to continue sleeping, and my tongue lolled out of my mouth in a proud wolfy smile. Curling my wolf around her body, I used my nose to tuck her against my side. With a whisper of a sigh, she twitched her tiny nose and nestled into my wolf's white fur.

Safe in the comfort of our home, I closed my tired eyes and allowed myself to sleep.

Chapter ELEVEN

SYRUS

I woke to the cutest sight I'd ever seen. The tiny gray bunny stretched her legs and yawned. Her large dark eyes blinked open, looking directly at me... then she released a terrified scream. Well, it would have been a scream if she'd been in her human form, but in her bunny form, it came out as an adorable squeak.

Bouncing to her paws, Monroe's gaze darted around the bed, pausing first on Cillian and then Rig. She looked ready to make a run for it. Cillian must have thought the same thing.

"Monroe. Calm down, sweetheart." Cillian remained motionless and kept his voice low and soothing. "You're safe. This is our home, and you are free to come and go as you please."

The tiny rabbit's heartbeat began to slow ever so

slightly, and her tiny pink nose wiggled. It was freaking adorable, and unable to stop myself, I licked her face.

Monroe squealed. Sitting up on her back feet, she used her tiny front paws to rub at the wet fur sticking up on her face. I snorted in amusement at the murderous scowl the puff of fluff directed at me.

"Syrus. That's gross, man. Keep it in your mouth." Rig yanked my tail, and then, reaching over me, he scooped Monroe up in his massive hands and cradled her against his broad chest.

Grabbing one of the soft blankets from the pile next to him, Rig wiped at the wolf slobber from her face. The drying fur stuck out at odd angles, and I huffed another laugh.

"Syrus! Go shift to your human form before I decide to enroll you in puppy obedience classes," Cillian ordered, pointing at the door.

Rolling my eyes, I made a move to obey, but changing my mind, I shifted to my human form. My completely naked human form.

Another tiny rabbit scream came from Monroe. Laughing, I grabbed the bunny from Rig's hands and cuddled her to my face. "Good morning, Puff!"

Indignant, she scratched at my face, trying her best to kick me away. Ignoring her efforts, I buried my face in her cashmere-soft fur and inhaled the fragrant jasmine scent that clung to her.

One minute I was cuddling the most adorable bunny on earth, and the next, I was being straddled by the sexiest woman on earth. My lungs forgot how to work, and I froze in shock.

"Would you cut it out?" Monroe growled. She was trying to sound mad, but there was no hiding the playful note in her voice or the way her mouth twitched in amusement.

Too stunned to speak, I choked on a chuckle. Apparently, that was the wrong thing to do.

Flattening her hands on my chest, Monroe shoved me, toppling us backward. Grabbing my wrists, she pushed my arms to my sides. She pressed her knees into my arms to keep me in place, pinning me against the mattress and freeing up her hands. She didn't need to try so hard, though, since I had no desire to 'get away' from whatever this was.

Still straddling my chest, she leaned in toward my face. And licked me.

Not waiting for a response, Monroe gave a husky giggle. "How do you like that, huh?"

Monroe's soft cheek brushed against my stubbled jawline as she nuzzled her face against my neck and began to murmur nonsense. I realized with shock she was teasing me and mimicking how I'd buried my face in her fur while whispering sweet nothings.

She sat back, a triumphant look on her face. "It's not so fun when you're cuddled against your will, is it?"

Cillian made a strangled sound, and when he spoke, his voice was low. "I don't think you made the point that you were hoping to make."

Monroe scowled at him before turning back to me.

I hadn't moved or even breathed. My skin burned with the memory of the brush of her breasts against my chest, her soft skin against my neck, the silky fall of her hair along my biceps, and the heat pouring from her core where it pressed against my abs.

My mouth had gone dry, and it took every ounce of control I possessed to remain pinned beneath her. I wanted Monroe, and having her naked body this close to mine was a temptation I wasn't sure I could resist much longer.

Monroe tilted her head and studied my expression. Her eyes widened, and she looked down at her naked body straddling my bare chest. A rosy blush tinted her cheeks, and she ducked her chin, allowing the curtain of dark hair to obscure her face from me. She made a move to get off me.

Not liking her pulling away from me and trying to hide her beautiful face, I growled. Sitting up quickly, I held her against me. Monroe's gasp of surprise turned to a breathy moan as her core slid down my abs and settled in my lap, where she discovered just how happy she was making me.

My hand traveled up the length of her neck, following the line of her jaw until I could grip her chin and tilt her face up to mine. "Don't hide from me, Puff."

Monroe's honey-brown eyes bore into my soul. Her shyness bled away, her pupils expanded, and her heart thundered as though she were running a marathon. Her sweet jasmine scent grew stronger, blending with a new note.

The exotic, sweet, and spicy fragrance was intoxicating

66

and caused my blood to pump harder. Brushing my thumb along Monroe's plump bottom lip, I leaned in. I was starving for a taste of her.

"Wait!" Monroe yelped, pressing her palms against my chest. Her eyes were wide with panic. "We need to talk, and time is running out."

I'd love to give her all the time in the world, but she smelled more incredible by the second. My rational thinking abilities were fading away, and my wolf was being stirred into a frenzy of need.

Clenching my teeth together, I ground out, "You better talk fast, Puff."

Chapter TWELVE

MONROE

Sweet baby carrots! How was I supposed to explain things while straddling a sexy and very naked wolf? There were so many things I wanted to do with him that involved our mouths, but talking wasn't one of them.

Monroe, focus! I gave myself a mental slap. Time was running out, and my heat was blooming... Ready or not, I needed to come. I glanced at the guys' faces, making my decision.

As much as it terrified me, I wanted them. And the truth was, I needed them. Desperately.

But first, I needed to give them the facts. Then they could decide if they wanted to run for the hills, and I'd use the last bit of time before my heat to find an abandoned burrow to hole up in.

Taking a deep breath, I plunged into my explanation.

"I'm about to go into heat, and I'm going to turn into a sex-obsessed bunny with a mind focused on just one thing."

All three guys' mouths fell open, and I would have laughed if the situation hadn't been dire. Whatever they thought I was going to say, this wasn't it.

Cillian opened and closed his mouth several times before managing to croak, "And this is a problem... why?"

I nearly facepalmed. Of course, he wouldn't understand the severity of the situation. He was a wolf, not a rabbit.

"You don't understand. This isn't something that is fixed by having sex a couple of times a day. A rabbit's spring heat turns her into an animal." I was trying to explain things, but it was hard to focus with my heat building steadily inside me. "It's the reason females are paired with a group of male rabbits. One or two male rabbits wouldn't be able to keep up with the sex drive of the female. We could literally breed them to death."

There was a shocked silence, and then all three wolves burst out into loud guffaws. Rig collapsed on the bed, grabbing his sides. Cillian tried, and failed, to straighten his features into a serious expression. Syrus squeezed me against him, his entire body shaking with laughter.

I crossed my arms under my breasts, only to blush when I realized I'd made them more prominent. Quickly readjusting my arms, I covered my breasts in a belated attempt at modesty. I'd always been shy about my appearance, but the heat had my body ready to beg for him to look.

Ignoring my inner hussy, I raised an eyebrow and tried to give them my best quelling look.

Syrus chuckled. "Puff, if you're trying to look intimidating, you'll have to try harder. Because right now, you just look adorable. And personally, the idea of being bred to death sounds like a freaking fantastic way to go."

"Quit calling me that," I grumbled. "What kind of nickname is Puff, anyway?"

"Sorry, no can do. The nickname is a done deal, Puff. It suits you perfectly because you're just a puff of fluff in your rabbit form." The corners of Syrus's eyes crinkled in amusement.

Maybe this was why rabbits didn't have relationships with wolves. Rabbits would never tell each other how cute they looked. Which makes sense, as we're all fluffy pint-size shifters when in our rabbit forms. Although, I suppose it was better for a wolf to think I appeared adorable rather than edible.

"Well, I guess that's better than looking delicious," I mumbled.

"Oh, I wouldn't say that." Syrus's mouth pressed to the pulse on my neck, sucking gently.

My body instinctually leaned into his heat, sending shivers racing through my body. Reluctantly pulling away, Syrus brushed his lips against mine. "You are definitely delicious."

"You know that since we're both in our human forms, that would be cannibalism, right?" I asked.

"It depends on which part of you I eat." Syrus winked, licking his lips.

"Is it just me"—Rig inhaled a long breath of air and groaned— "or is your scent getting stronger?"

That yanked me out of my lust-filled haze. "Crappity, crap, crap! You guys need to focus and let me explain things!"

"We're trying!" Syrus protested. "But you've got to quit telling hilarious jokes if you want us to take this seriously."

Exasperated, I threw up my hands. "It wasn't a joke!"

Syrus's eyes dropped to my suddenly uncovered breasts. Blinking furiously and with no small amount of effort, Syrus moved his eyes back up to meet mine.

"Okay, like I was trying to tell you guys before being so rudely interrupted." I narrowed my eyes, daring them to snicker. "You've heard the phrase 'breeding like rabbits,' right?"

The men's lips twitched, but to their credit, they didn't laugh. All three guys nodded their heads.

"That only applies to female rabbit shifters. A male rabbit shifter has the same sex drive as any male shifter. It's the females who go a little, well, crazy, every single time they go into heat. This is why female rabbits are paired with a large fluffle."

"A— What?!" Syrus's strangled voice reached an elevated pitch normally reserved for tween girls.

"A group of rabbits is called a fluffle—"

Syrus cut me off. "That's so freaking cute, Puff!"

Running out of time, I ignored him. "The larger fluffles are necessary to ensure that the female's needs are met while also making sure the males stay healthy... and alive.

Thankfully, our heat only comes a few times a year, and while every heat is awful, none are as bad as the spring heat. That one is always the hardest on a female rabbit."

I hesitated, nibbling on my bottom lip. "Especially when it's her first heat."

"And this is your first?" There was no laughter in Cillian's voice, and his expression was serious.

"Yes." My voice cracked.

"What do you need from us? Name it. We'll do anything for you, Monroe." Cillian caught my hand and gave it a reassuring squeeze. I hoped he didn't notice my sweaty palm.

My nibbling turned into full-blown chewing on my lip. Anxiety threatened to overwhelm me. All jokes aside, what I was about to ask them was a huge thing.

"Stop overthinking things, Puff. Just tell us." Syrus's hand rested on my bare thigh, and the rough texture of his thumb brushed along my skin.

"If I have to go through my heat, without... relief." I picked my words carefully. "I might not survive."

I wanted them to help me relieve the pain I would experience from my heat.

I wanted to ask them to take me as theirs.

But I knew I couldn't.

A female bunny's first heat bonded her with those males as her mates for life. Even if the wolves didn't get emotionally attached, I'd follow these men around for the rest of my life because being away from them would hurt too much. It's one reason what Seth had proposed to the elders was so terribly cruel. My heart would have bonded itself to them, but they would have been free to claim another female as their mate.

The same thing could happen with the wolves. When they claimed a worthy wolf shifter female as their mate, I'd be forced to watch from afar. It would break me.

Not waiting for their response, I rushed on. "Maybe if you guys have someplace where you could lock me up, that would work? Then I wouldn't be a danger to anyone... or to myself. There's a chance I could survive it alone. The older female rabbits taught us some tricks on how to find release. If I do it often enough and use some of the other techniques, I might be able to pull it off. The heat should only last about a week."

The flicker of hope eased a bit of the tension in my chest. I could do this. I'd survived the attack and survived years of cruelty at the hands of the rabbits. I'd done that by myself.

This would be just one more challenge I'd face head-on... and alone.

"Let me see if I understand. You want us to lock you in a room, ignore your pleas for sex, and listen to you pleasure yourself pretty much non-stop for a week?" Cillian's face filled with a comical mix of horror and incredulity.

"Yes," I whispered, because there wasn't another option for me. The rabbit shifters I'd been paired with all but rejected me as a partner, and I refused to live my life as their plaything.

"No," all three men answered as one.

74

Chapter THIRTEEN

MONROE

"That's the most logical option—" I pleaded, but was cut off by Rig.

"We said no. That isn't an acceptable option." He crossed his arms, his posture daring me to argue with him. "Not happening."

My muscles sagged in defeat. It probably wouldn't have worked, anyway. I couldn't survive the first spring heat alone. My eyes brimmed with tears.

"Why don't you tell us how your heat would've gone if you hadn't been matched with scum?" Cillian's voice was gentle.

Lifting my eyes, I met his gaze, cringing at the pity I saw there. How had he known about my matching? Come to think of it, how had they known to look for me in the woods?

"You know about Seth? And the others? But how?" My

chin wobbled, but I refused to cry. I'd been disgraced in front of the entire burrow; I couldn't ever show my face there again.

"The live stream of the event," Rig answered.

My heart lurched, panic and shame warring inside me. "You saw..." I stumbled over my words, trying to figure out how to describe the shattering of my entire world. *"That?"*

Cillian's thickly muscled arms wrapped around me, pulling me away from a protesting Syrus.

"Yes, I saw. I watched as one girl after another made their way into that room, each a near carbon copy of the other. And then I watched a woman step from the shadows. Her elegant dress clung to her in all the right places, making the statement that it didn't need the glittering adornments of the others."

Rig leaned toward us, and reaching out, he stroked my dark hair. "You were a queen among princesses."

I sucked in a ragged breath at the pride shining in Rig's eyes. They'd thought I looked beautiful. Desirable. Fresh tears burned my eyes as Cillian continued.

"Watching you walk between the tables was the worst torture I'll ever be forced to endure. Knowing at any moment you'd find your matches and be forever lost to me. It hit me with the force of a speeding train. I couldn't look away, but I also couldn't bear to watch."

Cillian held me cradled against his chest as he spoke, and I was surprised when something wet splashed my arm. Glancing up, I noticed the wet line a tear had traced down his cheek. Cillian was crying. Over me? Reaching up, I brushed my hand across his stubbled cheek, wiping away the evidence of his sadness.

"Then I saw you get matched with Seth. He's attended many business meetings, and I never liked him, but last night was the first time I thought about killing him. Seeing his hands touching your beautiful skin had me seeing red. When I saw your reluctance and realized he was forcing his touch on you, something inside me broke." Cillian's words became garbled, and I stared as his lips shifted to show protruding canines. He'd partially shifted.

I froze. It was the instinctual reaction of a prey animal realizing they were in danger.

Cillian's eyes widened. "Please, Monroe. Don't be afraid. I'll never hurt you."

And just like that, inexplicably, my fear bled away. I knew without a shadow of a doubt that I was safe with these men.

Not wanting him to worry, I pushed up onto my knees and wrapped my arms around his neck. There was no stopping a moan from escaping my throat at the erotic sensation of his bare skin against mine. The heat was already affecting me too much. It was supposed to ramp up slowly, not go from zero to sixty like a street racer from *Fast & Furious*.

"I'm not afraid of you, Cilly." I smiled at the nickname; it was perfect since he was acting silly. "If I feared you, don't you think I would have freaked out last night when you were in your wolf form?"

Cillian gave a jerky nod against my neck, and his warm breath sent goosebumps racing along my skin.

"Fine. I am a little afraid of you guys. Although it's mostly because of instinct," I confessed. Pressing my lips to his collarbone, I added in a whisper, "Somehow, that bit of fear makes me crave you three even more."

Cillian's body grew taut. "I want you. It's taking every fiber of my self-control to keep from taking your body right now. Please, tell us what you need before my wolf decides to take matters into his own paws."

Swallowing hard, I tried to collect my thoughts, but they were more jumbled than a kitchen junk drawer. All I could think about was the feel of Cillian's hand on my hip, how I wanted Rig to sink his fingers into my hair, and how I wanted Syrus to stop licking his lips and start licking other things.

Stabbing pain sliced through my stomach. Whimpering at the sudden onslaught, I doubled over and wrapped my arms around my waist.

"Puff?" Fine worry lines appeared around Syrus's eyes. "Are you okay?"

"Give me a minute," I wheezed. Closing my eyes, I breathed through the searing cramp until it subsided. "My body is giving me a not-so-gentle reminder that my heat is coming... and soon."

Pinching the bridge of my nose, I cleared my throat. "If we were going to do this here in your home, I'd require lots of snacks to keep up my energy. Access to a tub would be nice to help with the pain, but it isn't necessary. I'd also need to have a nest prepared."

Swallowing the lump in my throat, I thought about the room I'd prepared already. The room my rabbit bonded should have taken me to last night.

"Nest?" Syrus looked around the bed.

"This is one way rabbit shifters are a lot like actual rabbits. Females prefer fluffy nests filled with soft down. Rabbits will even pluck their own hair to line the nest."

All three men looked at my hair in horror, and I snickered. "I'm not going to yank out my hair to line the bed."

The wolves sighed in relief.

My stomach fluttered. I was asking too much. Sure, I was drawn to them, but technically, we were still strangers. Not to mention, was I seriously going to have sex with wolves? Would it even work? What if the heat could only be satisfied by male rabbits?

What if it was too much for the wolves, and I killed them with my insane neediness? I'd learned about anatomy in school, and most male rabbits weren't built like these hulking wolves.

Would our bodies even fit, or would they rip me in two? The thought of sex with the wolves had my skin tingling and my core growing slick. Clearly, my body was willing to take that risk.

"This is your room, and we can get you anything you need to redecorate it and make it yours." Cillian was typing feverishly into his cell.

I blinked, trying to get my mind out of the gutter and focus on what he was saying.

"I've got Brett headed to the store. What snacks do you want, Buns?" Rig glanced up from his phone with a questioning look.

"First Puff, now Buns? We need to have a talk about these names," I growled, and then tried to ignore Rig and Syrus's simultaneous 'aw' when my growl came out sounding more like a purr.

With no more time to waste, I rattled off a list of high-energy snacks, utterly embarrassed at the amount of food I was asking for. Rig didn't look surprised, though. He only nodded and typed the list to Brett.

"How can we make the room more comfortable?" Syrus asked. "If this was a burrow, what would it look like?"

"It would be underground, idiot," Rig scoffed, not bothering to look up from his phone.

Syrus rolled his eyes. "I'm aware, but I'm sure there is more to it than a hole in the ground."

"Yes. Being underground means it is dark. That helps to make us feel more secure. Soft lamps and candles would be placed around the room. I think if we add some more pillows and blankets, this will work perfectly for my nest." I patted the mattress. It was soft as a cloud; far plusher than the nest I'd prepared back in the burrows.

Syrus leapt off the bed and disappeared down the hallway. Less than three seconds later, he skidded back into the room, his arms overflowing with blankets in every color

80

and fabric. He tossed them onto the bed, burying me beneath them.

The sound of Cillian's deep laughter as he dug me out from the pile of fabric had butterflies taking flight in my stomach. He was effortlessly sexy, and I wanted to study his face for hours. I wouldn't, of course, since that would be creepy.

Unless I could find a way to do it without him noticing…

Chapter FOURTEEN

MONROE

I was pulled from my stalker-ish musing when another sharp burst of pain rattled my insides. Grinding my teeth together, I barely managed to keep from screaming.

Cillian looked up from his phone, his eyes searching my face. I quickly schooled my face into a blank mask, not wanting to alarm the guys. I just needed a few more minutes, and then I could stop fighting against my rising heat.

"Everything is on its way. Now you need to explain how we can best tend to your needs." Cillian spoke as though he were arranging a meeting with a client rather than asking me to describe in detail all the kinky bunny business that was about to go down.

A white-hot twinge of pain in my abdomen had me gasping. Catching my breath, I plunged ahead with my explanation. "My heat will come on fast. First, I will get really, um, needy. If that isn't taken care of, then the pain will hit me full force. Not just waves of pain, but constant agony. The only way to ease the discomfort is for me to orgasm. The more often I orgasm, the less pain I will feel. This is why fluffles generally have at least five males. It gives each male a little longer to recover between matings."

Without realizing it, I'd begun to chew on my lip again. Rig's large thumb touched my lower lip, drawing my attention to the abuse I was inflicting on it.

"Calm down, Buns. We are more than capable of meeting your needs without kicking the bucket. You are seriously underestimating our stamina. I'm confident we could give the rabbits a run for their money when it comes to sexual prowess. Who knows, we might even outlast you." Rig winked.

His sexy bedroom voice left me panting, and warmth flaring inside me. It was a flame that grew hotter and more out of control with each passing second. Time was running out.

"I hope you're right," I mumbled, picking at a loose thread on the blanket. "I'd never forgive myself if my horniness caused a homicide. What if all my copulating creates complete carnage? What if I do you in while I'm doing you? I'd never forgive myself if I caused a mating massacre!"

All three men howled with laughter, still not comprehending the serious risk they were taking. They were the ones underestimating the stamina of a female bunny in heat. I made my way to the edge of the bed, preparing to crawl out and go find a hole to hide in for the next week.

Syrus gave me a soft smack on my bare butt before pulling me onto his lap. "Puff, it's a risk I'm willing to take. Besides, I like challenges." Syrus nipped at my earlobe.

"There is more to it than that." Sex was one thing. What I had to confess next was just as worrisome. "The problem is that my rabbit may bond to you guys during the week. I promise I'll do my best to avoid it, but it is nearly impossible to prevent. Female rabbits love caring for their mates, and our hearts tend to attach to the men caring for us during our heat."

I couldn't meet their eyes. "You don't have to bond with me or claim me, though. And if I bond with you, I'll try to stay away and not be clingy." I rushed to add the last bit, hoping to reassure them.

Rig caught my chin and turned my face to look up at him. "What if we want to claim you?" he asked.

I sucked in a breath. Rig's normally guarded face was open, allowing me to see he was serious.

"Yeah, I don't remember any of us saying we didn't want you to claim us," Syrus added. "I'm still not seeing a downside to your heat."

Cillian stole me away from Syrus. Wrapping his arms around me, he held me in a tight embrace. "You stole our hearts long ago, and our wolves claimed you as theirs. We were trying to give you space and not force you into a relationship with us."

Tears welled in my eyes, relief bursting like a dam inside

me. "I didn't want you to feel like you didn't have a choice."

"We had a choice. We chose *you*." There was no hesitation in Cillian's words.

They chose me.

They wanted me.

They thought I was worthy of being their mate.

Joy erupted inside me, and I opened my mouth to tell them how much it meant to me, but instead, a scream ripped from my throat as pain slammed into me.

A sheen of sweat coated my body, and my stomach twisted, causing liquid agony to fill my abdomen. My breasts grew heavy, and the dull ache between my legs intensified.

I was out of time. Ready or not, my first spring heat had arrived.

The men were shouting words at each other, but my brain no longer cared to listen. All I could think about was the way my body hurt. With each wave of heat that ricocheted through me, my body was left vibrating with a need so powerful it drowned out all thoughts except one. *Sex.*

Unable to help myself, I ground my hips down against Cillian's lap and moaned at the delicious friction. For a fraction of a second, the pleasure eased the pain that was tearing at my insides like a rabid squirrel. However, the moment I stopped moving my hips, the heat returned with a vengeance. Tears left wet trails down my cheeks as I cried over the intense pleasure and then the crippling pain.

"Do you smell that?"

I wasn't sure who spoke; their words seemed to be spoken underwater and a million miles away. Shifting my hips again, I moved my slick heat against Cillian, and once again, the pain was pushed back slightly.

Cillian held me against him as he rose on his knees before laying me gently down on the bed beneath him. Hovering over me, he pressed his face to my neck, slowly kissing his way down between my aching breasts. His tongue was warm as he lapped at my skin. It felt different from how I thought it should, and glancing down, I studied him.

He was still human, but also not quite human.

Cillian's eyes were glowing orbs—the eyes of his beast. His lip curled up slightly, and I caught sight of his sharp canines. Those fangs were meant to tear into flesh, but Cillian was using them to tease my sensitive skin.

When his tongue curved around my nipple, I whimpered. He'd partially shifted his tongue as well, and it was much longer than a normal human tongue. Dirty thoughts of what I wanted him to do with that tongue had my body burning with need and embarrassment.

Sinking my fingers into Cillian's hair, I held him to me, savoring the abrasive texture of his tongue against my skin. He took his time, using his enhanced tongue to curl around and tease the hardened peak of my nipple. To my shame, I felt my body hurtling toward climax. How could this happen with nothing more than his tongue on my breasts?

Cillian pulled back, breathing hard. His arms, which were braced on either side of me, shook slightly. Through heavy-lidded eyes, I watched his eyes roll back into his skull.

"I've never tasted anything so sweet. I must be crazy." Cillian blinked hard, then his predatory eyes focused on me. "You taste like sugar?"

My mouth had gone dry, and I struggled to speak. "Ye-yes. When I'm in heat. It's supposed to make you want me more."

His face took on a wild look. "Do you taste like sugar in other places?"

I didn't get time to answer before Cillian slid down my body and settled himself between my parted legs. He didn't give me time to prepare before his tongue plunged deep inside me.

The sudden penetration had me clawing at the bed in an attempt to get away from the brain-frying sensation. Cillian grabbed my hips, refusing to let me escape. He continued to sink his tongue deep inside me, lapping up my cream like a starving man... or animal.

Rig and Syrus moved to either side of me. Syrus lowered his mouth to my breast, teasing and licking. Rig's mouth captured my lips in a demanding kiss. Cillian apparently didn't appreciate sharing and gave the two men several warning growls... which they ignored. His rumbling growls sent vibrations through my core, and it was more than I could handle.

I screamed his name as my world exploded in an earth-shattering orgasm.

Chapter FIFTEEN

MONROE

The need and pain should have eased with my orgasm, but instead, both intensified. "Please," I begged. "It hurts."

Slipping my hand to the junction of my thighs, I tried to touch myself, only to have Cillian bat away my hand with a snarl.

"Let us tend to you." The words were layered, as though two people were speaking at the same time instead of one.

"Are you okay?" I panted, trying unsuccessfully to focus on his face.

"He's fine. His wolf is fighting him for control. They both want to claim your body, and neither one is willing to sit in the background," Syrus whispered while his tongue traced along the edge of my ear.

I didn't care who did the claiming, so long as they got on with it. Again, I tried to slip my hand between my legs, desperately searching for any type of relief, only to have Cillian snatch it away with a warning growl.

Anger surged through me. "Either help me or get out of my way!" I snarled. "You said you wanted me? Then show me!"

That seemed to do the trick. Cillian yanked off his sweats, his thick erection springing free. Another wave of slick heat coated my core at the sight of him, and I whimpered. Cillian slid a hand down his length, giving it a hard squeeze.

My body trembled as another cramp rolled through me. "Please," I begged, my eyes blurring with tears.

Cillian lined himself with my entrance, pausing only for a moment before burying himself inside me. He was far larger than any of the toys that were designed to look like a male rabbit shifter's erection. A new type of pain shuddered through me.

"Don't hurt her, Cillian!" Rig growled.

"Back down!" Cillian snarled at Rig, who responded by grinding his teeth together.

Cillian's eyes locked onto mine, his face tense. "Are you okay, Monroe? Do you want me to stop?"

"I'll die if you stop. And then I will come back to haunt you, and I'll spend the afterlife ruining your sex life. I'll be the ultimate erection deflection," I gritted out.

In response, Cillian slowly eased himself deeper inside me until I felt the head of his erection press against my cervix. My fingernails dug into his arms as another wave of agony ricocheted through me. Desperate for release, I squirmed against him.

"Be still." Cillian moved his hips, slowly easing out of my tight channel. It was an exquisite combination of torture and pleasure. "I've got you."

My heat protested the emptiness by causing my muscles to cramp and spasm. I couldn't even speak for fear I would scream. Cillian must have realized that while his gentleness was thoughtful, it was causing me more pain.

"I'm sorry," Cillian whispered before burying himself deep inside me.

I saw stars as he picked up his speed, each thrust faster and harder than the one before. I clung to him, my body hurtling toward my next climax. The world around me burst into blinding light, and I forgot how to breathe as ecstasy poured through me like molten lava.

My body clamped down on Cillian's erection. He groaned and his body stiffened. I moaned when he jerked inside me before collapsing on the bed beside me, his eyes closed and breathing erratic.

I wanted to enjoy this beautiful moment, the first time I'd felt Cillian in me. But the demanding pain of my heat eased for only the span of two breaths before it threatened to swallow me in agony all over again. I cried out, rolling onto my side and curling into a tight ball. The room swirled, and my stomach lurched. I was going to be sick. This was too much. How was I going to survive this much pain for days on end?

Warm hands slid beneath me, lifting me off the bed.

Syrus tucked me against his body. He brushed my hair away from my cheek, and craving his touch, I leaned into the roughened palm of his hand.

"Puff, look at me." Syrus's voice was gentle.

With immense effort, I opened my eyes to peer up at him.

"Focus on me, honey. Let me take care of you, okay?" Emotion swirled in Syrus's eyes.

"Okay." I rasped out the single word, unable to manage more than that while my body seemed to be actively attempting to rip my organs in two.

Syrus moved to the raised edge of the bed, where he lifted me to sit on the beautiful painted wood floor. He shifted onto his knees, positioning himself between my legs and lining himself up with my entrance.

I closed my eyes, hunching into the scorching heat of his body as another agonizing cramp scrambled my insides.

"Look at me. Focus on me, Puff." Syrus tilted my face up to look at him.

The tight worry lines around Syrus's eyes and mouth broke my heart. Our first time together shouldn't be like this. But there was nothing I could do about it now.

I did my best to blink back my unshed tears and focused on Syrus. The swollen tip of his erection pressed against me, sending a thrill of desire weaving its way through my misery. If this heat planned to kill me, I'd die content.

Not willing to wait, I wrapped my legs around his waist and pulled our bodies together. We groaned in unison. His erection wasn't as long as Cillian's, but it was thicker. I wasn't sure he would have fit inside me had he been my first partner that morning.

The movement of Syrus sliding against my tight walls was enough to ease some of the heat's pain… at least momentarily. But as soon as he stopped moving, my insides began to ache. I bit my lip, needing more but unsure how to ask.

The older women had taught us that as the heat progressed from the early stages, female rabbits became bolder about taking what they desired. I wasn't sure which was more embarrassing… having to ask, or being greedy and taking what I wanted.

"What do you need?" Syrus leaned down, sucking my bottom lip between his.

My body arched into his. Tightening my legs, I held him tight against me. "More. Faster. Harder."

Great. My vocabulary had been reduced to single words. Frustrated, I tried again. "I want everything, Syrus. Don't hold back."

Those words were all it took for the sweet boy-next-door guy to melt away. Syrus pulled his hips back in one swift move. I didn't even get a chance to protest his absence before he'd sheathed himself inside my slick core. Hard.

His hungry mouth moved down my neck, and his tongue stroked my feverish skin. "You taste delicious, Puff. Addictively sweet." He groaned, his thrusts becoming rougher.

Trembling, I clung to him, delirious with need. Each roll

of his hips sent a new wave of ecstasy crashing through me, washing away some of the pain.

"More, Syrus." My fingers traced the lines of his abs, enjoying the way they flexed as his pace increased. Both our bodies were slick with sweat. The animalistic need for release had driven away all other thoughts from our minds.

We moved as one, our bodies rocking in perfect rhythm to a song only we could hear. The coil of lust inside me sprung free, and my climax shuddered through me. Syrus's hands slid under my thighs. His fingers dug into my skin as he lifted my hips and angled me so he could drive his erection deeper into me.

"Syrus!" I purred his name, shocked to realize my need had already begun to build again.

I tilted my head to the side, giving Syrus better access to my neck. It was an instinctual move, and one I hadn't thought all the way through.

The last thing a prey animal would ever do around a predator was to show them their neck. It was the equivalent of putting out a sign that said 'eat here' while ringing a dinner bell.

So I shouldn't have been surprised when Syrus's teeth sank into my neck. It wasn't a cute little love nip, either. Oh no.

This bite was savage, with both his upper and lower teeth slicing through my skin.

That was when all Hades broke loose.

Chapter SIXTEEN

MONROE

I screamed. Not from pain, but from the violence of my orgasm and the almost instant relief from my pain. It wasn't gone, but it seemed somewhat satisfied and had quieted to a level I could survive.

Rig and Cillian's growls echoed off the walls of the room, and the raw power of the sound made even the tiniest of hairs on my body stand on end.

"Release her!" Rig snarled.

"Syrus! Don't. You. Dare," Cillian warned, punctuating each word with a snarl. I caught his eyes over Syrus's shoulder, surprised to see rage and murder glinting in the green orbs.

I wanted to ask what Cillian didn't want Syrus to do. Bite me? Frankly, with Syrus's teeth deep in my neck, it kinda seemed like he had already 'done the doing' that Cillian was warning him against.

Syrus jerked and stilled. He still held my thighs, clamping my body tight to his groin.

Cillian's hands reached out for me, preparing to pull me away, but Rig stopped him. "Cillian, stop. It's too late."

"That doesn't sound good—" I was cut off as Syrus's erection, still deep inside me, did the impossible. It grew thicker and longer. There was so much pressure—too much. Panic surged through me. My body wasn't made for males this large!

Tears burned in my eyes, and I tried to push away from Syrus. My body was too full, and my walls burned as they stretched. This pain had nothing to do with my heat and everything to do with the monstrous erection I was impaled on.

"Be still, Buns. If you pull away now, it will cause more damage." Rig's large hands caught my smaller ones, keeping me from shoving against Syrus's chest.

"He's going to rip me in two!" I cried.

"No, he's not. Let your body relax; it will adjust to him." Rig's normally rough voice had dropped to something akin to a purr, and my body responded instantly.

As soon as I quit struggling and allowed my taut muscles to relax, the pain grew more bearable. With each breath, the pain caused by his size warred against the pain of the heat, until they almost canceled each other out. I let myself relax a little more.

Rig kissed the tops of my hands. "Good girl."

"Wha—How?" I wasn't even sure what to ask.

Cillian answered, his face a dark scowl. "Syrus claimed

you as his mate. The idiot bit you while being inside you. That triggered the mating shift... and I'm going to kill him for it."

"Mating shift?" My voice cracked, and my eyes widened. If he shifted into a wolf with his mouth on my throat, would he remember that he liked me and resist the temptation to eat me?

"Calm down, Buns," Rig soothed. "He's not turning into a wolf. Wolf shifters are gifted with some enhanced abilities we can also use in our human form."

I nodded woodenly. Rabbit shifters had a few tricks up their sleeves, so it made sense that other shifters would as well.

"One of those abilities is triggered by biting while having sex. Our"—Rig's cheeks reddened, and he coughed awkwardly—"penises expand more than a human male, and the base grows thicker. This locks the couple together until the swelling goes down."

Despite the pain, joy burst through me. Syrus wanted me, not just for tonight, not just as a toy to be played with, but as his lifemate. After the humiliation of the rabbit reception, I'd feared I would never have mates or a family of my own. While these men had said they wanted me as theirs, Syrus had gone a step further than words. He'd shown me with his actions.

Shifting my hips, I tried to find some relief from the overwhelming fullness I was experiencing. I wasn't able to move more than a few centimeters, though. Rig wasn't kidding about us being stuck together. Which sucked because the cramps had begun again, and I knew I didn't have long before the pain would return full force.

"Impetuous pup," Cillian growled under his breath.

Rig snorted. "He's twenty-two. That's hardly a pup anymore, Cillian."

"Then he should stop acting like one," Cillian snarled.

Their squabbling faded into the background as the swollen base of Syrus's erection rubbed against my most sensitive bundle of nerves. Rolling my hips again, I gasped when he rubbed me in just the right way. Lust flooded every nerve ending in my body.

I found my pace, and using those few centimeters of wiggle room, I rocked his engorged erection against my g-spot. Cillian had brushed against it when he was thrusting into me, but that didn't compare to the delicious pressure massaging me as Syrus was at that moment. Panting, I moved faster, my heat driving me to use his body to satisfy my needs.

Syrus growled, my neck still clamped gently in his mouth, and the vibrations rumbled down my throat. I wasn't sure if he was warning me or encouraging me, but as desire boiled my blood, I didn't care.

Everything inside of me was on fire. A delicious heat that licked every nerve ending in my body. One last roll of my hips, and I screamed in ecstasy. Syrus grunted, his erection twitching inside me. I wondered if he was more sensitive while swollen and made a mental note to ask… later.

As the aftershocks of my orgasm faded away, so did my cramps, giving me complete relief from the pain of my heat.

The rabbit women had talked about the rare occasion that a female's mates may be able to satisfy the heat enough to give her a period of relief amid her heat. But it was a talent so rare it was considered a myth among rabbits. Was it possible that Syrus had discovered a way to ease the heat's strain on my body?

Syrus's teeth eased away from my neck, and his tongue licked along the punctured skin. Light-headed and trembling, I fell against his chest.

When Syrus finally stopped licking my neck, I lifted a hand to evaluate the damage. To my surprise, I found only raised welts. There was no blood or open wounds, only healing scars. It was one more thing I needed to ask him about. Later. All I wanted to do at the moment was sleep.

"My sweet little Puff." Syrus's husky whisper caused my heart to flutter as he held me against him.

Several minutes later, the swelling receded, releasing our bodies from the lock he'd created. But he still didn't let me go, and I didn't want him to. My eyes fluttered closed, and I cuddled deeper into Syrus's arms, relishing the soothing body heat of my mate.

"I can't believe someone wants me... that I have a mate." I kissed Syrus's bare chest.

"You have more than one mate, Buns. I can't wait until you also wear my mark on your beautiful skin." Rig lifted me from Syrus's lap and strode down the hallway. He gave me a quick but heated kiss on the lips. "I have a bath ready for you. I've put some herbs in the water. It'll help with pain and any injuries Syrus might have caused."

Cillian's voice came from behind us. "Syrus will pay for putting his mark on you before me. But I'll deal with that later."

"Worth it!" Syrus shouted from the sunken bed.

Rig's chest rumbled in laughter at Syrus's cocky response.

I peeked over Rig's shoulder to see Cillian carrying a tray overflowing with snacks and every conceivable flavor of sports drink. He winked at me, and a tender smile played across his lips. Tears burned the back of my eyes. They were so thoughtful, and they anticipated my every possible need.

Happiness bloomed in my chest, along with something else.

I'd been attracted to these men for months, but what I felt now was more than that. I was falling head over cottontail in love with these three wolves.

My wolves.

My mates.

Chapter SEVENTEEN

MONROE

W e cuddled in the bed together after my bath, with Cillian stroking my hair while I relaxed against him. I'd nearly fallen asleep when he said, "What would happen if you bonded with mates who didn't claim you back?"

Anxiety wormed its way through me, and my breath hitched. "Honestly, I've only heard stories of it happening, and it was miserable for those women. They could never move on and find a family because being too far from their bonded mates hurts like a mother-trucker. And what sucks even more is how the pain worsens every time the males she's bonded to are with another woman. It isn't just an emotional pain, either. The cheating causes physical pain so severe that it usually leads to the female being hospitalized."

Cillian's fingers trembled in my hair. "And Seth was going to do this to you? Did he know what it would do to you when they allowed you to bond with them but then took another female as their chosen bonded?" His chest rumbled like a thunderstorm as he spoke.

"Yes," I whispered, my voice cracking. Seth would have loved causing me pain for the rest of my life.

"Wait. He'd knowingly cause you that kind of pain for the rest of your life? And the elders were willing to go along with it?" Rig's fingers dug into the mattress. He must have partially shifted because an ominous ripping sound followed.

Now didn't seem like the best time to go into detail about Seth's past treatment of me, so I tried to stay vague. "Seth always felt entitled to toy with me, and as the son of an elder, it has always been overlooked."

"Syrus, watch her. Rig, come with me." Cillian all but threw me at Syrus before bounding off the bed and storming out of the room with a snarling Rig hot on his heels. A few seconds later, the front door slammed against its frame hard enough that the entire house trembled.

"What's going on?" I asked, eyes wide as I stared at the empty doorway the men had exited through.

"Wolf business," Syrus purred.

I was sitting on his lap again, but this time facing away from him. Syrus's hands glided down my body, and even though I was confused by Rig and Cillian's abrupt disappearance, I moaned.

Arching back against him, I delighted in the sensation of his bare skin brushing against mine.

"Do you want me to stop?" Syrus hummed against my ear, his palms sliding up my belly to cup my breasts.

"Noooo." Groaning, I ground my hips into his lap.

I went cross-eyed when his stiff erection jerked against me. My belly burned, growing heavy with lust.

"Maybe we should wait for the others to come back?" Even as I spoke, I reached my hands behind my head to sink my fingers into his hair and keep his lips against my skin.

"Or maybe we should enjoy this time with just the two of us?" His teeth sank playfully into the back of my neck—in the precise spot a predator might bite to snap their prey's neck.

A tendril of fear unfurled in me, but instead of fight or flight mode kicking in, the threat of danger excited me. Syrus was unlocking something in me, and I wanted to get my freak on with him.

I tried to turn in his arms to face him, but he gripped my hips and held me in place on his lap. Syrus shifted beneath me, and my body trembled as his hard erection slid along my slit. He wasn't trying to bury himself inside me; he was teasing me.

"Syrus." I moaned and squirmed, desperate to feel the delicious friction again.

"Patience, Puff." He gently nipped the skin where my neck met my shoulder. "We have all the time in the world."

I growled, which only made him chuckle. Giving in to

my wiggling, Syrus shifted his hips, stroking his velvet length against my sensitive folds again. I dropped my head back against his shoulder, reveling in how incredible the simple movement felt.

I'd been taught how to take care of my own sexual needs, but it was nothing compared to being touched by a man. *My man.*

Syrus continued to suck and nip my neck, his hips lazily moving as he teased me. With each stroke, I grew increasingly slick, lubricating him until he slid smoothly against me.

When an intense sugary taste filled my mouth, followed by Syrus's deep inhale and a long suck against my neck, I knew the heat was continuing to accelerate at lightning speed.

The deluge of hormones from my heat was working like a toxin, affecting every part of my body. Over the next twenty-four hours, not only would I continue to be a needy mess, but the heat would subtly shift my outward appearance as well.

During each heat, my skin would glow, my lips would grow plump, and my hair would shine like I'd just been to a celebrity salon. All to ensure my bonded would find me impossible to resist. As if that wasn't enough, there was the sweet taste the wolves had already noticed.

Female bunnies had a sweetness to their skin all the time, it was an odd quirk. But when the hormones from the heat flooded our body, our skin went from a hint of sweetness to tasting like a five-star dessert. Even our sweat was affected, turning into an aphrodisiac men found addictive.

"Monroe." Syrus groaned against my neck while his tongue continued to lick the sheen of potent hormonal cocktail from my skin.

Concern trickled through me. It was intended for male rabbit shifters, and we didn't know the effect a large dose might have on a wolf. I opened my mouth to warn him, but Syrus's hand sliding along my inner thigh cut off anything I would have said.

When his fingers teased my aching slit, my body trembled violently. "Please." I didn't care that I was begging. All I could think about was his touch and the release I desperately wanted.

Syrus didn't make me ask twice. He slipped a finger into my slick core. I rocked against his hand, trying to find friction. Giving me what I wanted, Syrus slid a second finger inside me and ground his palm against my soaked entrance.

All the while, he continued sucking and lapping at my skin like a man starved. I needed to tell him to not ingest so much until we could figure out the effects, but I didn't want him to stop.

"I need to feel you in me. Please, Syrus." Raw lust had turned my voice husky.

Syrus didn't respond, but in a single smooth move, he rolled me onto my back beneath him. Using his muscular thigh, he wedged it between my legs, opening them to him.

He jerked his hand along his hard length and lined

himself with my entrance. But before he could thrust himself inside me, the house shook, and a bellow echoed down the hall.

The roar was feral and sent a tendril of fear skating down my spine. It was an erotic duo, and my body responded by sending a rush of desire straight to my core.

Chapter EIGHTEEN

MONROE

I was jerked from my lust-filled haze by the bedroom door flying open. It slammed against the wall hard enough that the handle embedded itself into the drywall.

Cillian and Rig stormed into the room. Both men were shirtless and wore only their dark sweatpants. Their chests were covered in scratches, as though they'd just had their butts handed to them by a rabid alley cat.

Rig's expression was sullen, his facial muscles jerking as he clenched and unclenched his jaw. Cillian's eyes were wild as he scanned the bedroom for a threat. Both men froze mid-step as their minds processed the scene in front of them.

"What is going on?" Cillian bellowed.

"We were about to do some parallel parking until you so

rudely burst in" didn't seem like the most polite response, so I reigned in the out-of-control lust that threatened to choke me and asked a question of my own. "Where did you go? And what in the deviled eggs happened to you two?"

Rig mumbled something under his breath and shot a sour look at his shirtless companion. Cillian's lip curled in a smile, and I caught my breath. He looked powerful and dangerous... like a sexy demon who'd just caused mischief.

"Cillian?" Syrus's thoughts must have echoed my suspicions. "What did you do?"

Ignoring him, Cillian strode to the bed and sank down next to me on his knees. He moved closer until my chest was pressed against his, and our lips were only millimeters apart.

"After hauling Rig's impulsive butt back to our territory, I made a few calls." Cillian's long fingers played with my hair as he spoke.

"We were having sex and cuddling, and you suddenly remembered you needed to make business calls?" I asked, unable to hide my incredulity. Turning to Rig, I added, "And you needed a run? If you don't want me here, Rig, I'll leave. This is your home."

My heart ached at the thought of leaving, but I would never want to force these men to endure my presence. Rig settled against the pillows opposite me, his sharp gaze trailing along my exposed body. Still, he said nothing.

Cillian rolled his eyes. "Rig has an issue with controlling his temper, and when that happens, his wolf often gains control. His wolf decided he wanted to hunt down a particular rabbit and see that immediate justice was served. I couldn't trust Rig while he was in wolf form, so I forced him to shift back to his human form. The thickets are full of thorns, and we both got scratched up on our way back."

My eyes widened. Rig's eyes shot daggers at Cillian's back.

"Why'd you stop him, Cil? Seth deserves everything Rig would have dished out!" Syrus's arms wrapped around me, pulling me against him... and away from Cillian.

The shift happened so fast I thought I was hallucinating. One minute Cillian was human; the next, he was— I didn't know what he was. He was neither man nor wolf.

No, he was something in between.

Werewolf.

Wait. Those weren't real, were they?

"Dude! You are going to terrify her!" Syrus shouted, his hand covering my eyes in a belated attempt to keep me from seeing Cillian.

I batted away Syrus's hand and watched as the wolf-man-thing opened his snout-mouth-thing and spoke. My mouth dropped open, and my brain struggled to comprehend the strangeness of this monstrous beast speaking English.

"Don't ever pull her away from me, pup. She's mine." Cillian's lip curled, flashing his very sharp fangs at Syrus.

Syrus stiffened behind me, but to his credit, he didn't cower away from Cillian version 2.0. "She's ours too. Get that through your thick skull!"

For a moment, I thought there was going to be a fight,

but finally, Cillian nodded his head a fraction, acknowledging Syrus's words. "Fine. *Ours.*"

Cillian took another minute to calm himself before continuing. "And to answer your previous question, Seth will pay dearly for his treatment of Monroe. But a quick death is too merciful. Which is why after I hauled Rig's impatient pelt home, I made a few calls."

Cillian's glowing green eyes locked with mine. "We have a treaty with the rabbits."

"I know." I resisted the urge to roll my eyes. Everyone knew that.

"Part of that agreement requires the elders to ensure there is fair treatment among the rabbits. Wolves do not tolerate inequalities within their community, and we didn't want to protect a society of shifters who failed to protect their own members from being hurt and abused, emotionally or physically."

My heart stumbled, losing its steady rhythm. Surely this wasn't going where I thought it was going...

"The elders have been notified that our treaty is now void due to their treatment of you. I have already pulled my security. They are no longer patrolling the land around the burrows."

"Frick yeah! That's why you're the man, Cillian!" Syrus whooped and leapt to his feet. Holding me tight around the waist, he did a weird victory dance.

I peeked at Rig from the corner of my eye and caught the devilish smirk that slid across his face. Tears blurred my vision, and I struggled with my warring emotions.

After years of suffering abuse and neglect in the burrows, it felt amazing to have revenge. But I'd also been proud to be a rabbit shifter, and until last night I'd wanted to honor my parents' memory by doing my part to make the burrows stronger. Yet now, because of me, the burrow was as weak as it had been when the coyotes attacked.

This was impossible. There was no way he'd managed to do all this in the few minutes he'd been gone.

"How? How are you able to do all that?" I asked. Was he that well respected among the wolves that he could get the wolf shifter's alpha to do as he asked?

Cillian's ears twitched, and his brow raised. "Do you know who I am? Who we are?" His features had softened from rage to amused curiosity.

How was I supposed to know who he was? I knew his name and his coffee order, but that was about it. I was on the lowest rung of the burrows' social ladder. Actually, I probably wasn't even on the ladder. The elders weren't inviting me to attend the rare wolf and rabbit meetings, nor did I have a close group of friends to gossip with.

I'd owned a small television when I was younger, but Seth and his friends had stolen it. I spent every waking moment working, so I didn't exactly have time to keep up with the who's who in the shifter community.

I was a loner. Shaking my head, I waited for his answer.

Cillian's voice was tender. It was an odd contrast to his ferocious features. "Baby girl, I *am* the wolf alpha. Rig and Syrus are second and third in command over the pack."

My blood didn't just turn cold, it froze in my veins.

He was the alpha.

THE FREAKING WOLF ALPHA?!

Chapter NINETEEN
MONROE

I *'d had sex with the alpha wolf.*

Reality hit me like a two-by-four to the face. If he was the alpha, it meant what he'd said earlier was true. The burrows were completely unprotected. And at the worst possible time. Most of the men would be busy caring for the bonded females who were going through their spring heat. Tears rolled down my cheeks.

"Why are you crying, Monroe? Are you afraid of us?" Cillian's monstrous form bent over me. "Of me?"

I should have been afraid of them. They weren't just wolves; they were essentially wolf royalty with strength beyond what regular shifters held. But I didn't fear them—not even Cillian's werewolf form scared me.

"I'm not afraid of you. It's just, I don't want the rabbits to die because of me." I sobbed as the dam holding back my emotions broke.

"I cannot forgive how they treated you, or for the life they were willing to curse you to live. The rabbit elders are already blowing up my phone with requests for a meeting. They want to discuss a new agreement, and I fully intend to arrange that meeting after your heat is over."

I wrinkled my brow, not understanding why he was making them wait. "I'm sure Syrus or Rig could stay with me for a little while so you could meet with them."

Cillian gathered me in his arms and settled down onto the lush mattress that was piled high with blankets. "Beautiful, as long as Rig keeps his wolf under control, nothing is going to drag me away from you again. If the rabbits want something from the wolves, the rabbit elders will need to come begging on their knees for you to forgive them."

"BEG ME?" I shouted before quickly covering my mouth in embarrassment.

Cillian smirked. "Oh yes, and they better come ready to plead for your help. Otherwise, I will throw them out. Whatever arrangement you wish to agree to, I will honor. I am yours to command, little rabbit." Cillian's words had fresh tears running down my cheeks and dripping onto his chest.

He respected me and wanted to make me happy. I hadn't felt respected in my entire adult life. It was incredible, but it didn't stop me from worrying.

"I can see the wheels spinning in your mind. You're still upset. What would you have me do?" Cillian growled.

I needed time to think about what I wanted, but now was not that time.

Not while hormones were pumping through my blood, and my heat was clouding my judgment and fogging my mind. My body had been temporarily sated, but now I needed rest and food—and not necessarily in that particular order.

But I also didn't want the rabbits to be wiped out while I was caught up in satisfying my lust.

"Can you ask your wolves to protect the rabbits until the meeting? Maybe from a distance, so the rabbits don't realize you're still guarding the burrows?" My voice trembled. I had no right to ask anything of this man... the alpha.

"Rig," Cillian barked. He tossed his phone toward the beta wolf, but his eyes never left mine.

With a sigh, Rig caught the phone and tapped at the screen for several seconds. Once he'd finished, he powered down the phone and placed it on the hardwood floor. "Done."

A wolfish smile spread across Cillian's face.

"I know that look, Alpha. Shift back before you mate her," Rig said.

Cillian rubbed at his head, snarling in frustration. He paced the wood floor beside the bed. "Don't you think I would if I could? My wolf won't back down. We are both maintaining half control, which is why I'm in this form."

"Fascinating," Syrus whispered, his chin tucked on my shoulder. "You've only ever held that form for a couple of minutes at a time in the past."

"Yeah, well. It requires a level of equal willpower from both my wolf and myself. We've never had anything we both wanted badly enough to fight over before. He wants her just as much as I do." Cillian's gold eyes glinted. How could such a fearsome creature look so gentle?

I pushed away from Syrus, crawling across the bed to Cillian. He'd sat down on the wood floor at the edge of the bed. Cillian remained still, waiting to see what I was going to do.

I paused, gathering my courage. Up close, his beast was huge. As a man, Cillian was around six-foot-five, but in this form, he was close to eight feet tall. Which made my short stature look completely ridiculous next to him. Was I even tall enough to ride this ride?

I felt inside for my rabbit, expecting to find her desperate to escape. She was desperate, all right. But not to escape. Oh no, my horny inner bunny wanted this hulking beast.

I pushed myself off the mattress and climbed onto the floor with as much grace as I could muster. Sliding a leg across his lap, I groaned when the width of his thick, muscled thighs forced my upper thighs to spread in a near split.

Cillian's fur was thinner than when he was in his full wolf form, but there was still a significant amount of fur. It should have felt weird brushing against my skin, but it tickled and teased my bare skin as I adjusted myself on his lap, sending goosebumps traveling the length of my body.

Still unmoving, Cillian watched me with interest and a hint of worry in his eyes. There was something else in their depths, and it caused my stomach to clench. He was still worried I was afraid of him... and that I might reject him. I slid my arms as far around his chest as I could.

"You said I was yours?" I whispered, rubbing my cheek against his soft fur.

"Yes. You're mine." Cillian's words were thick, and his chest rumbled.

"That means you are mine, too?" I reach a hand up to tease his ear, longer than a human's but shorter than a wolf's. Cillian moaned, his chest trembling. It seemed I'd found a sensitive spot.

"Yes. Please let me be yours." Cillian's words were so soft I almost missed them.

My heart cracked at the longing in his voice. The monster alpha wanted me to claim him as mine. He was offering himself up to me. A rabbit.

All doubts and hesitation melted away until all that was left in me was lust and a tiny but bright flame of love. It needed time to grow, but it was there. I'd begun falling in love with them. "Mine," I whispered, a magic word that changed my life like a fairy tale spell.

Chapter TWENTY

MONROE

My body trembled as we neared the conference room doorway—a room filled with the burrow's rabbit leadership. If it hadn't been for the three wolves pressed against my back, I would have bolted back the way we'd just come.

While my heat had eased in the last four days thanks to my mates' constant attention, it wasn't quite over. But I didn't want Cillian to keep putting this meeting off. Especially since the rabbit elders had become more demanding in their requests for a meeting with each passing day. I didn't owe them anything, but I also didn't want the entire burrows to suffer because of the decisions of a few Grade-A jackrabbits.

Syrus gave me a gentle shoulder bump. "You've got this, Puff."

"Don't worry. If they so much as look at you wrong, I'll eat them." Rig winked.

His teasing words did little to ease my anxiety—probably because I wasn't a hundred percent sure he was joking.

"Remember, they can't lay a finger on you without facing my fury." Cillian leaned down, placing a gentle kiss on my cheek and pressing his hand against the small of my back.

Straightening my spine, I lifted my chin and stepped into the alpha's conference room.

Shock rippled across every face in the room, but I did my best to keep my expression smooth and unbothered. As expected, the seven rabbit elders were present, as well as five of the rabbit shifters who guided the burrow's businesses and commerce.

The remaining five rabbit shifters were faces I'd not planned to see ever again... in this lifetime, anyway.

My unmatched-matched-bunny-bonded.

To be fair, they didn't look any happier about seeing me. It was the clear disgust and rage on their faces that sparked a fire in my belly. I wanted them to be angry. For once in our lives, I wanted them to have to actually listen to me and treat me like a human instead of their plaything.

My wolf mates led me through the plushly carpeted room to the head of the long mahogany table. Every seat had been taken except for the three leather chairs at the farthest end.

Rig and Syrus grabbed the two seats on either side of

the largest chair, which was clearly meant for the alpha. Realizing there wasn't a chair for me, my heart accelerated. Memories of being publicly humiliated year after year flashed through my mind at the speed of light. Surely the wolves wouldn't bring me here just to embarrass me.

Catching my hand, Cillian pulled me down on his lap. He tucked my loose hair behind my ear and leaned in. "Don't doubt me again, little mate. We are not like the rabbits."

My belly flip-flopped at his sexy growl, and I reminded myself to keep it together until the meeting was over. The last thing I wanted was to start ripping his perfectly tailored dark suit off...

"If you keep looking at me like that, I'm going to end the meeting before it begins and kick everyone out," Cillian whispered.

My cheeks burned, and I was thankful when he turned to address the rabbit shifters.

"Normally I would open this meeting by saying, 'Good morning, gentlemen.' However, it is not a good morning since, if not for this meeting, I would be relaxing in the comfort of my home. I also do not consider any of the men at this table gentleman, after what I witnessed of how you have treated women in the burrows." Cillian's voice was cold as ice, and his eyes held a predatory glint.

Bunny instinct should've had me making a run for it, but I sat up straighter on his lap. The mate bond was growing stronger with each hour, and knowing the big bad wolf had my back was proving to be a powerful confidence booster.

"Thank you for seeing us, Alpha." Bernard, one of the elders, bowed his head as he spoke. "But with all due respect, why is *she* here?"

Cillian lifted a brow. "Do you have an issue with Monroe being here?"

"I understand that you are unhappy with reports of mistreatment in the burrows. Although, let me assure you, there has been a misunderstanding. And we are thankful you found one of our lost females. Her bonded have been distraught over her absence, and we will happily reimburse your pack for any inconveniences you incurred due to her misadventure."

Cillian's body was vibrating against mine, and the arm of Rig's chair creaked ominously under his grip. The elder didn't realize the danger he was in and decided to dig his hole deeper.

"Monroe is a female, and her only job experience is as a waitress. She doesn't possess the needed skills to be of value in this discuss—"

That's as far as Bernard got before Rig was at the opposite end of the table and lifting the man from his chair. Storming to the door, Rig tossed Bernard out of the room and slammed the door closed in his stunned face.

"Unless you wish to be thrown out like Bernie the Bunny, I suggest the rest of you choose your words carefully," Rig snarled as he returned to his chair beside me.

"You can't just throw him out!" Frank, a second elder, made a move to stand.

Cillian gave a dark chuckle. "I own this building and most of this city, so yes, it is up to me who stays and goes. Sit or leave; I don't care."

"As you wish, Alpha." Frank agreed and took his seat. I didn't miss the way his jaw tightened when he looked at me.

A quick glance around the table told me none of the rabbit shifters present were happy to see me.

Taking a moment to compose himself, Frank began. "We would like to assure you that the burrows care deeply for every rabbit living there. The televised portion of the ball was out of context and dramatized to get higher views. We treat all rabbit shifters with equal care. It is unfortunate that emotions got a bit out of hand."

My mouth fell open. How could the man sit here and lie straight to our faces? Every rabbit in the room knew and had turned a blind eye to the mistreatment I'd received. They hadn't cared when I'd been in elementary school and had returned home after school each day with torn clothing from being roughly pushed around the playground. The elders had buried the school nurse's report that I was undernourished from having my lunches stolen every day.

The only thing that changed when I went to middle school was that the bullies increased their efforts to make my life terrible. The elders once again did nothing when my clothes in the locker room were cut to ribbons while I showered after PE. They ignored my dropping grades due to my assignments 'disappearing' after I turned them in to the teachers.

High school was the worst of all. My bullies knew they could get away with anything short of killing me, and I became the butt of every cruel prank the other students could think of. Seth and his gang made sure I was put on their team for every group project, so they could leave me to do all their work—just like I was forced to do the rest of their homework.

When they'd sabotaged my science project, causing it to explode and embed shrapnel in my skin, I thought the elders would finally punish their sons for the cruelty. Instead, they suspended me for endangering my classmates intentionally. If I hadn't been a shifter, I would likely have suffered vision loss and long-term damage from their 'prank,' but I was the one punished.

I would never forget the smirking faces of Seth, Zane, Malcolm, Tom, and Jordy as they stood behind their fathers as I was being punished. They had won, and there was nothing I could do.

Once I graduated, I'd believed they'd leave me alone. But they'd gone out of their way to continue their harassment. How many cups of scalding hot coffee had they spilled on me and then complained to my boss over my clumsiness? I'd lost count.

Then there were the nights they would stand outside my window shouting drunken insults until the wee hours of the morning. My things were constantly going missing or being destroyed. The worst was the times they would barricade me in my room and leave me trapped until someone heard my calls.

Lost in my thoughts, I jerked when Syrus's voice brought me back to the present. "If that is true, then what would have happened if Monroe had stayed at the ball?"

"She would have received the same care as every other female rabbit as she navigated her first heat," Sam, a third elder, snapped.

"I see. So she would have spent her heat with her matched mates, and they would have bonded with each other. I understand that is customary during a female's first heat." Cillian's tone was flatter than a ghost's pulse, as though he was completely uninterested in the conversation.

I wanted to speak up, but my tongue refused to move, and so I did what I'd always done when dealing with these rabbit shifters—pull into myself and try to guard my heart so their words wouldn't hurt as much.

"Well, uh, not quite," Sam stammered.

Rig rested his palms on the table and leaned forward. "Yes or no? Was the fiasco on the television part of some soap opera, and Monroe's matched males—your sons— were going to bond with her during the first heat?"

Seth was turning red, and I could hear his knuckles cracking beneath the table. He was livid and barely maintained control of his temper.

"Monroe didn't give us time to explain things to her. Yes, the boys were going to bond with her when she went into heat."

Seth stood so fast his chair toppled to the floor. "What the frick, Dad! You swore we could pick a girl next time and wouldn't be stuck with the loser. I can't believe you'd lie to me!"

Rig growled, and this time, he didn't walk around the table. No, he jumped onto the table and slid across it to slam into Seth with a sickening crack. Blood gushed from Seth's nose as Rig hauled him off the floor and threw him into the hall as though Seth weighed nothing more than a pillow.

"You attacked him for no reason!" Sam shrieked in outrage.

Rig stopped mid-step, turning on his heel to face the man. "I attacked him for many reasons. He's lucky he escaped with only a broken nose."

Somebody help me! Either my heat was flaring up, or the temperature in this room just spiked 15 degrees. Sweat trickled down my spine, and my core clenched as I watched the intimidating wolf shifter do what I'd wanted someone to do for me all my life... stand up for me.

Cillian sniffed, and he must have smelled my arousal because I felt him grow hard beneath me. This meeting needed to hurry itself along, or we were going to have a serious problem.

Chapter TWENTY-ONE

MONROE

Sensing we were running out of time before the next bout of heat pain hit me, Cillian spoke. "Let's cut through the crap. You don't care about Monroe, and you treated her as nothing more than a commodity. We clearly have different ideas of what protecting and caring for our own means."

"That's an insult!" Frank spluttered.

"It's the truth, and you will shut up and listen," Rig snarled, his muscles flexing beneath his suit jacket.

"Here's the deal. I want nothing else to do with the burrows. I do not want to be contacted with your issues or concerns. I do not want to receive calls regarding business ventures you want me to invest in. I do not want rabbit shifters working in my office buildings and handling important wolf documents. I do not want to continue to pay my wolves a salary to guard the burrows. I am finished, and I will not reinstate the previous arrangement." Cillian was eerily calm as he spoke.

Pandemonium broke out among the rabbits. Outcries of breached agreements and unfair treatment were thrown at Cillian. For his part, Cillian looked amused.

When the elders realized that the wolves hadn't responded to any of their arguments, the room descended into an awkward silence.

"Are you finished?" Cillian asked.

The elders ground their teeth and nodded.

"Good. Then I will continue. You asked me to reconsider. I did, and I still refuse to uphold the old agreement or create a new one. The only reason we are sitting here today is that Monroe doesn't want the burrows unprotected. Because of her request, we have continued to guard the burrows until this meeting could take place."

Every set of eyes in the room stared at me.

Cillian wasn't finished blowing all our minds. "If you want a new agreement with the wolves, you will need to get her approval. Any further business you wish to have with me will be through her."

What in the Timothy Hay was he doing? The rabbit shifters didn't respect me, so why would he think making me the liaison between our two species was a smart idea?

Sam found his voice first. "Alpha, this is extremely unfair. We are willing to work within your terms, but we request that we be allowed to choose who is our delegate to work with you."

128

I needed to find my backbone. The wolves were standing up for me, yet I was sitting here like an idiot.

"No." I was shocked at how strong and firm I sounded, and by the looks on the faces around me, I wasn't the only one surprised.

Cillian's arm tightened slightly around my waist, giving me an encouraging squeeze. Drawing on that simple gesture of strength, I pushed ahead. "I am your only option, take it or leave it. Right now, I am the only reason the burrows are still protected, so I would suggest you reconsider your attitudes."

"Can we have a moment to discuss this privately?" Frank asked, directing the question to Cillian.

With a sinking feeling, I realized these men weren't ever going to change their attitude toward me. My hands began to tremble, and anger burned in my belly. That led to a new problem. It seemed my heat reacted to fury in the same way a fire reacts when you pour gasoline on it.

Boom.

I stood to my feet, flattening my palms on the table and leaning toward the men, channeling my inner boss babe. "You can have the next two hours to discuss it. We have things to attend to and will visit the burrows to gather my things. I'll look over your proposal there."

Frank opened his mouth but shut it really quick when all three wolves rose to stand behind me.

"You can see yourself out. My mate has told you her terms, and we have nothing left to say." Cillian's voice had lost the bored, unaffected tone he'd maintained the entire meeting. He sounded *very* affected as he dropped that truth bomb.

My suspicions were confirmed when his arm slipped around my waist, and he pulled me back against him. Our significant height difference caused his hard erection to press into my back.

The first ripple of pain whispered through me, a precursor to the racking cramps that would come if I didn't find relief quickly. How was I going to make it to the house before then?

"YOUR MATE?" Sam and Frank bellowed.

"Our mate," my three wolves answered together.

That was the moment the rabbits lost their cocoa-puff crap.

"This is unacceptable!"

"A rabbit cannot mate with a wolf!"

"This is disgusting!"

Syrus and Rig shifted in spectacular harmony. Rig leapt onto the table for a second time, his massive wolf stalking down the mahogany table toward the outraged rabbit shifters. Meanwhile, Syrus was making his way down the side of the conference room, herding the rabbits toward the door like a collie herding sheep.

"Then I suggest you leave quickly unless you wish to hear something truly unholy. Because I am about to worship my luna's body and satisfy her heat." Cillian used his wolf's rough voice. Looking up, I watched his sharp canines descend, and his eyes begin to glow.

I should've been embarrassed that he'd just told them he

was about to breed me, but all I felt was pride. Seth and posse had thought I wasn't worthy of being their mate. Now I was mated to the alpha wolf, and he wanted me. I was the luna and the person they needed favors from.

This was my moment.

How do you like me now?

Wanting them exactly how much the alpha had wanted me, I brushed my hair back over my shoulder, allowing his marking bite to be seen. Tilting my head, I presented my neck to Cillian—showing them how much I trusted him.

My mate responded instantly to my submissive gesture. Leaning down, he kissed the mark on my neck before gently nipping it. The scrap of his teeth across my skin sent heat rushing to my core, and I swallowed a moan.

The last thing I saw before Rig's body slammed the door closed was Seth's furious expression.

Then I forgot everything as Cillian kneeled behind me. With a low growl, he lifted the skirt of my sundress over my hips, exposing my butt and tiny pink thong to his hungry gaze.

"How do you smell so incredible? It was all I could do not to bend you over this table and take you on the spot, not caring who was watching." As Cillian spoke, he gently pushed me forward until my elbows and forearms were bracing me on the table.

In this new position, I was presenting myself to him like a female in heat... which, to be fair, I absolutely was. When Cillian pressed his mouth against the tiny strip of fabric covering my aching core, my body arched off the table.

Cillian chuckled. His tongue traveled just under the edge of my thong, teasing me, before he stood.

"You should have skipped the thong. It's in the way." His fingers brushed down my burning skin as he removed the silky garment, letting it fall to my ankles.

He unbuttoned his perfectly pressed slacks, and a heart-beat later, his hard length pressed against me, seeking entrance. Cillian's hands gripped my waist, angling my hips to give him better access. Our extreme height differ-ence would have made this position impossible if not for the oversized conference table.

My stomach spasmed, and sharp pain burned like light-ning through me. It seemed my heat was done being patient. Biting my lip, I barely kept back a scream.

"Hurry. My heat… it hurts," I whimpered between waves of pain.

Cillian didn't hurry.

Pushing forward, he eased inside me, inch-by-excruciat-ingly-slow-inch. Cillian's thumbs gently stroked my back as he held my hips. The tenderness of the gesture had tears springing to my eyes.

I was in the alpha's opulent conference room, on his private floor that overlooked the city, at the top of the wolf shifters' business headquarters. He'd exposed me and posi-tioned me on the table for his pleasure.

Everything about this was dirty and naughty. Yet he wasn't pounding into me looking for his quick release. The big bad alpha was making love to me.

It was heart-stoppingly romantic... and abso-freaking-lutely frustrating!

"Cillian," I growled. "This isn't a go-slow-and-enjoy-the-scenery moment. This is a bang my bunny brains out type of moment!"

Syrus and Rig guffawed, but Cillian responded by leaning down and nipping my neck. He meant it to be playful, but my heat viewed it differently.

"Ohhh." The raw moan ripped from my throat as my body arched off the table. "Cillian."

"Crap man. Either give her what she's begging for, or move and let me." Rig's gravely rumble made my core clench.

Cillian groaned. "She's so tight, and your voice is turning her on more."

I opened my heavy eyelids to look over at where Rig leaned against the wall.

"By my voice?" Rig seemed shocked, then a dark look that promised all sorts of wonderful things settled over his features. "Is that right, Buns? Does my voice make you want to do dirty things?"

Rig had dropped his pitch an octave lower, and combined with the wicked smirk, it was too much. My entire body quivered, and a sheen of sweat coated my skin.

Cillian buried himself inside me, but I was so tight that it was a challenge, even though I was soaked. His breathing was harsh, as he worked to thrust in and out. As our bodies rocked together, I looked over at Rig and Syrus.

Syrus was relaxing on the floor, while Rig still leaned

against the wall. My jaw hit the table when I saw what they were doing. They'd freed their stiff erections from the confines of their slacks, and were stroking themselves while watching their alpha pound into me.

It was sexy as heck to know my mates were that turned on just by watching. I couldn't take it anymore and my release exploded through me. Cillian followed me into bliss, burying himself deep and locking us together.

My heat retreated, once again sated by my mates.

Chapter TWENTY-TWO

MONROE

I decided I wanted to take a shower and put myself back together before we drove out to the burrows. Truthfully, I was just trying to put it off. As much as I wanted to be a confident luna with a backbone of steel, I was a bunny.

Confrontation wasn't something I'd ever be able to handle well. Even now, I'd guarantee the elders were discussing how to manipulate this situation to their advantage.

Sighing, I stepped into the little black dress I'd picked to wear. It had been tucked among the closet full of clothing, shoes, and accessories I'd woken up to the previous day.

I may not have experience wearing designer garments, but I could recognize them. Heck, they even smelled expensive! But my stubborn mates had refused to return any of it, claiming they'd waited years to have a mate to spoil.

The black dress was the perfect blend of take-no-prisoners boss and let's-do-something-naughty succubus.

Stepping out of the bathroom, I laughed when my three mates began to pant—in their human forms.

Syrus led me to a fluffy white vanity chair and gently brushed my hair. Rig picked a pair of high-heels with dainty straps that laced up my calves. Kneeling in front of me, the big bad beta slipped them on.

Cillian handed me a box.

"What's this?" I brushed my fingers across the black velvet.

"Why don't you open it and find out?" Cillian teased.

Nervously, I lifted the lid and stopped breathing.

A glittering tiara was nestled on a silk cushion.

"It's the luna crown," I whispered in awe.

You didn't have to be a wolf shifter to recognize the iconic accessory. My mother was an artist who had been fascinated by the stunning piece. The tiara was famous for its intricate design of swirling white gold and countless diamonds that sparkled like stars in the night sky.

But it was the precious gemstone shaped like a crescent moon that was featured prominently in the middle that was the stuff of legend. The wolves either didn't know what it was made of, or they weren't telling, and the mystery had created an almost cult following in the paranormal community.

Since the luna crown was rarely seen and even more rarely photographed, the mystery was nowhere close to being solved. In person, I was disappointed to see the moon held only a dull glow, though. Maybe the photos of the brilliantly glowing stone had been photoshopped?

Looking up at Cillian, I batted my eyelashes and teased, "I don't suppose you will tell me what makes the crescent moon glow?"

Syrus leaned forward and whispered conspiratorially, "The alpha's love."

It was so dramatic and silly I laughed—only to stop when I realized the guys weren't laughing with me.

"I don't understand?" I reverently traced the delicate edge of the tiara.

Cillian scooped me up in his arms and carried me to an oversized chaise lounge that sat in the corner next to a large bay window. Sitting me down on his lap, he brushed a kiss against my cheek before plucking the tiara from the box.

"Syrus was telling the truth. It's the alpha's love for his luna that gives the stone power. The moon goddess gave this stone to the wolves. It's meant to be a physical reminder for the luna of her mate's love—even when he is being a temperamental beast and utterly unreasonable." Cillian's smile was sad.

"My father was the last alpha to touch the stone, and that was many, many years ago. Both of my parents passed away nearly thirty years ago, and yet his love was so strong, the moon still holds some of its glow."

Unshed tears sprung to my eyes. "I'm so sorry, Cillian. I know what it's like to lose your parents. It's a wound that never heals."

We were quiet, and then he spoke again. "It was a long

time ago, and this is meant to be a happy moment." Cillian kissed my cheek. "Now it's time for my luna to wear the crown."

My heart stumbled, then screeched to a halt. He wanted me to wear the wolves' heirloom? "I'm not a wolf shifter, though."

"That doesn't matter to me. Nor does it matter to any other wolf. You are their luna, and that's all they care about." Finished speaking, Cillian pinched the moon-shaped stone between his thumb and forefinger.

I watched in awe as his fingers began to glow—no, not his fingers. It was the moon that radiated light. When Cillian moved his hand, the centerpiece of the crown was awash in a beautiful, buttery glow.

"That's incredible!" I breathed. And then it hit me.

The stone glowed from the alpha's love.

Cillian loved me?

He must have read my expression because he carefully placed the tiara on my head and then captured my face between his calloused palms.

"I love you, Monroe. My heart belongs to you for the rest of our lives. You are everything I could have hoped for in a mate and so much more." Cillian captured my lips in a searing kiss that turned my body to jelly.

"My turn." Rig yanked me from Cillian's lap, lifting me in his arms.

I yelped in surprise, and my dress rode up to my hip as I wrapped my legs around his waist.

"I thought I could live happily without a mate, but that

changed the morning you walked out to take my order for the first time. It tore me apart to think you might not ever accept a wolf as your mate, and now I will tear anyone apart who tries to take you from me. You're mine, Buns. I love you." Rig brushed a featherlight kiss across my lips, and before I could react, he strode to Syrus and dumped me in his lap.

It was the weirdest game of pass the potato I'd ever played, but I was one thousand percent living for it.

"Hello, Puff," Syrus purred, his voice husky.

"Hi." My cheeks warmed. All I could manage was a lame *hi*?

Syrus chuckled, nuzzling my neck. "In case you didn't know, I'm in love with you."

"Really?" Was this really happening? I chewed on my lip. "It's so soon. How can you guys love me this fast? Maybe it is just a side effect of my heat?"

All three wolves growled.

Syrus rubbed his nose against mine. "Puff, your heat is one heck of an incredible bonus, and I never thought sex could be so mind-blowing. But we loved you before your heat started."

Rig snorted. "Yeah. You don't actually believe we like that trash coffee at the café, do you? The only reason we kept coming back was to be near you."

"Shut up, Rig! You're making us sound like creepy stalkers," Syrus snapped.

Rig shrugged. Ignoring him, Syrus continued. "We were devastated when we saw you being matched at the reception. But you are ours, and we will never let you go. Never."

"Now who's being creepy?" Rig grunted.

My heart was so full I thought I'd burst at the seams. "I don't think it's weird, I think it is amazing. It's been so long since I'd felt loved. This is everything I've ever wanted."

Tears of joy streamed down my cheeks, and the storm of anxiety inside me calmed. It didn't matter what happened at the burrows because I had everything I could have ever hoped for. I belonged to and was treasured by these men.

I was loved.

Chapter TWENTY-THREE

MONROE

As the car neared the burrows, my heart banged around in my chest like a drunken seagull. I'd never wanted to come back here again.

When the elders delivered their cruel verdict at the ball, with nearly every bunny in the community present to witness my humiliation, I'd run from the main hall. In the dressing area, I'd been greeted by several of the female bunnies who'd been matched in previous years.

Cruel laughter and insults weren't the only things they hurled at me. A few of them had thrown their wine glasses and splattered my beloved gown with the dark red liquid.

The elders' decision had cemented my status in the burrows. I was lower than an omega in the wolf community. Watching the stains bleed through the gray silk of my dress, I'd been devastated. Then I'd had a moment of crystal-clear clarity.

I'd never find love, or even acceptance, within my community.

Pulling my eyes from the all too familiar scenery flashing by the car window, I ran my thumb across the fabric of my black dress. It was fitting.

Forget being a black sheep; I was the black bunny of the burrows.

The car slowed, coming to a stop at the beautiful tree-lined path that led through the burrows to the main building. There were a few buildings in the burrows, and these acted as entrances to the underground tunnels that had housed most of the rabbits since the coyote attacks.

The trees were in full bloom, creating an archway of pink and red blossoms. It was amazing how tranquil and sweet everything about our community looked on the outside, completely hiding the toxicity lurking beneath the surface.

Rig opened my car door, and, holding out his hand, helped me from the car. Syrus stepped out behind me and adjusted my skirt before I had a chance. Cillian stepped to my side. Tucking my arm through his, he led me down the petal-covered pathway.

"Just let me know if I can kill anyone for you," Rig whispered from behind us.

"There won't be any killing today." I hesitated, thinking of Seth's angry face when he'd been kicked from the conference room, and added, "Probably."

"Yesss," Rig hissed. "That means there's a chance."

A real smile spread across my face... until I glanced down the nearly football-field-length path and spotted the angry faces waiting for us outside the main house. The elders must have gathered nearly every rabbit in the burrows. They wanted to make sure I knew how hated I was among my kind.

It was a blatant attempt to intimidate me.

Despite my determination to be confident, my legs wobbled, and I missed my step. I would have fallen if not for Cillian's steadying grip on my arm.

"Keep your head up, Luna." A man I didn't recognize strode past me. Turning, he gave us a wink. "We've got your back."

"We?" Perplexed, I watched him leap into the air, his clothes shredding as he shifted. When he landed, it was on the cinnamon-colored paws of his wolf. I stared in shock. He'd shifted with the effortless grace and smoothness of an elite athlete.

"Thank you, Brett," Cillian rumbled.

"Show off," Rig grumbled.

Brett lifted his shaggy wolf head and howled. It was hauntingly beautiful, and goosebumps skated across my skin. In the distance, a wolf answered. A third wolf responded, then a fourth and a fifth. Within sixty seconds, I'd lost count of how many wolves were joining in Brett's eerie howl. Was it twenty? Forty? A hundred?

Not all the howls were in the distance, either. It seemed like many were coming from the woods that surrounded us. That was confirmed when wolves began to stalk from the shadows where they'd been lurking. Several moved to walk alongside Brett's wolf.

The rest of the massive wolf shifters remained on either side of the path, bowing low to the ground as we passed between the two walls of wolves. Peeking over my shoulder, I watched wolves with coats of gray, cream, brown, copper, and black pour into the pathway behind us.

"How many are there?" I asked reverently, never having seen so many wolves in my entire life.

"Six thousand nine hundred and sixty-nine," Cillian answered without hesitation.

I choked. "But how? There aren't that many wolves living in our small town."

Cillian stopped walking, smiling down at me. I turned to face him, and he pulled me against his body.

"I'm not only the alpha over this town, Monroe. My land and wolves stretch across the US. These wolves represent only a small part of my pack."

"Why are they here?" I whispered, although I knew every wolf within a mile radius probably heard me.

Cillian chuckled. "For you. They're here for you."

My lip wobbled, and I blinked hard, determined not to cry.

"The wolves have a luna for the first time in decades. They've been arriving in town over the past several days, hoping to see you." Pride and love shone in Cillian's eyes. "I'd already ordered my guards to be concealed in the woods today. But Brett's howl was a call to arms, and every

wolf in hearing distance responded. They dropped everything to be here."

I was losing the battle. A tear trailed down my cheek.
"But I'm a rabbit. I'm not a wolf shifter. They're okay with
that?"

Cillian wiped away my tear. "You are part of our pack
and part of our family. On top of that, you are their luna.
Wolves protect each other—emotionally and physically.
These wolves will protect you with their lives. Not because
I ordered them to, but because they want to."

Catching my chin between his thumb and forefinger, he
tilted my chin up. His lips met mine, and he kissed me like
we were the main characters in a Nicholas Sparks movie.
My ears rang with the happy barks and celebratory howls
of the wolves around us.

Pulling away, I smiled at the smear of pale pink lip gloss
on Cillian's lips. Going up on tiptoe, I wiped it from his
mouth. "Let's do this, Alpha."

This time, when Cillian led me down the path toward
the now nervous-faced rabbits, I positively floated. For the
first time in my twenty-three years, I was walking through
the rabbit shifter community with my head held high, no
longer trying to hide.

I wasn't afraid. Why should I be? I had an army of
wolves at my back who accepted me.

The rabbit shifters had made a mistake.

*They'd thrown me to the wolves, but I'd come back... leading
the pack.*

Chapter TWENTY-FOUR

CILLIAN

y head was throbbing, but I refused to let the pain show on my face. Saying the wolves were happy to have a luna was the understatement of the century. The pack was buzzing with energy and exuberant joy.

Are you going to be okay, Cil? Rig asked through the link, knowing full well the toll this was taking on my body.

As alpha, I had a telepathic link to every wolf in my pack that was within about ten miles. Unlike an individual wolf who could choose who to open a link with, the link between each pack member and me stayed open so I could hear any cries for help.

Normally, this wasn't an issue since only a few hundred wolves lived in the town. Right now, there were a few thousand wolves all sharing their thoughts in my mind. My head felt like it was going to explode as white-hot agony crackled through my brain, but I was happy to deal with the pain so that Monroe would see the pack's devotion. I could sleep the pain off later.

My little mate glanced up at me, her brow wrinkling as though she were trying to figure something out. Hesitating for a moment, she let go of my sleeve. Ducking under my arm, she pressed herself against my side, letting my arm drop to her shoulder.

Her hand snuck under my jacket, where she untucked a small section of my white dress shirt in the middle of my back. My mate's palm pressed against my bare skin.

Cool relief flooded through my head. It was like aloe on a sunburn. I turned wide eyes on Monroe. How had she known I was in pain?

She gave me a sweet smile and kept her hand on my back. To onlookers, it would appear she was being affectionate. It took all my control to resist throwing her over my shoulder and taking her back home, where I could worship this little angel for the rest of the night.

"Alpha."

We'd reached the end of the path, and the rabbit elders dipped their heads in respect to me. I didn't miss that they ignored my mate, and neither did the pack.

Brett crouched, baring his teeth. The wolves began to growl, and with so many snarling wolves crowded in and around the burrows, the ground vibrated beneath our feet.

The rabbit shifters began easing away from the elders. All except the males Monroe had been matched with. They stayed behind their fathers, shooting angry looks at my mate.

Realizing their dismissal wasn't going to be tolerated, the elders gave a clipped, "Luna."

"Elders." Monroe's tone was regal, like a queen meeting her subjects.

I wanted to laugh, but with effort, I managed to school my features into an expressionless mask.

"Follow us, please." Elder Frank motioned for us to follow him.

He led us to a clearing like something from a storybook. Oversized, rough-hewn picnic tables with matching benches were scattered around the grassy lawn. The elders moved to the largest table in the middle of the clearing. Rig, Syrus, Monroe, and I settled across from them.

The rabbit shifters in the clearing moved to claim seats at the other tables, effectively surrounding us. It was a tactical move on the elders' part. They wanted to throw us off balance with a show of force.

Sure, if both species were shifted, a single wolf could take out every rabbit in the clearing. But with all of us in human forms, we were outnumbered and would have a challenge fighting our way out.

Well, we would have been outnumbered if not for my pack. I wasn't the only one who'd seen through the elders' little mind game. The large wolves weaved between tables, spreading out to provide backup if needed. The rest of the wolves created a wall around us.

The elders watched the wolves, eyes tightening as they

watched their plan backfire. Instead of showing us their strength, all they'd done was show every rabbit in the burrows how weak they were. If I wanted them dead, I could snap my fingers, and the rabbits would be wiped out in less than five minutes.

They needed us. We didn't need them. And every tense face around us showed that they definitely knew it.

To my surprise, Monroe didn't wait for the elders to speak first. "Have you created a proposal for my consideration?"

I shifted slightly on the bench, covering my mouth with my hand to keep from smiling. Monroe wasn't playing around anymore.

"Yes, we have, Monroe." Elder Sam slid a document toward her.

"Luna." Monroe didn't reach out to take the paper.

"Excuse me?" Elder Sam's face wrinkled in confusion.

"Not Monroe. It's Luna to you. None of the elders cared to remember my name in all the years I lived in the burrows. You don't get to use it now. We aren't friends."

This time, Rig was the one scrubbing his hand across his jaw to hide a smirk. She might shift into a bunny, but she had the courage of a wolf.

Sam ground his teeth, struggling to control his temper.

Elder Frank decided to step in. "Of course, Luna." He slid the paper closer to Monroe.

She said nothing but reached out and turned the paper toward herself. Monroe began to read. Her face darkened as a storm brewed inside her the further she read until I could practically feel the lightning crackling around her.

"I'm going to focus on the main points." Monroe clasped her hands on the table. "First, you want us to increase the number of guards around the burrows at no cost to the community. Second, you want a rabbit shifter to have a seat at the table during all wolf shifter meetings, even if only wolf business is being discussed, although you aren't offering a reciprocal seat for a wolf to attend all rabbit shifter meetings."

Syrus dropped his head into his hands at the rabbit elders' audacity.

Monroe wasn't finished, though. "Third, since all werewolves in the pack receive a small monthly stipend from the profits coming from werewolf-run businesses in town, the elders wish for all rabbit shifters to receive the same."

As hard as I tried to resist the urge, I snorted. These rabbits had lost their crap.

"Oh, and what about number four?" Monroe held out her fingers, ticking off points. "You want the wolves to agree not to interfere in rabbit traditions and customs, even if they find them morally questionable."

I narrowed my eyes at the shifters across the table. Had they even tried to sound reasonable? Perhaps this was a prank? If that were the case, the joke would be on them. I despised pranks that wasted my time.

"Did I understand all that correctly?" Monroe asked, her tone cold.

The elders nodded their heads.

"All right, so let's talk about what it is you plan to do for your end of the contract, shall we?" Monroe pretended to check the paper. "First, you agree to provide each member of the burrows a private one-hour meeting each year to express their concerns."

"Yes, the alpha expressed his annoyance that we weren't aware of your feelings. This would ensure, in the future, every rabbit gets a chance to speak with us and isn't too intimidated to approach us."

Let me kill him. Please? It can be an early birthday present? Rig begged in the mental link.

Yes, let Rig kill him. It can be my birthday gift too, Syrus pleaded.

I fought my wolf. He wanted to let Rig spill blood. *Hold it together. If Monroe gives the order, you are free to obey her. Otherwise, let her handle these men.*

"I see." The muscle in Monroe's jaw twitched. "Let's move on to the other three items. Two, you will provide councilors to speak with unmatched female bunnies to ensure they are fully prepared for what to expect at the ball and how to best represent the burrows during the televised event."

My eyes shot to Monroe's face. She had to be joking.

"Third, the rabbit shifters will continue to work in wolf establishments to keep the town running, but at a ten percent higher wage."

Hades! I already paid every rabbit working within the town's limits nearly twice the minimum wage, and bonuses. And we didn't need the rabbits to staff our businesses. We could easily provide those jobs to humans or provide more work for the wolves.

"And finally, point number four. You will accept me as liaison, under certain conditions." Monroe kept her chin up and her back straight. "We made it very clear back in Cillian's office that I'm the only liaison you will get. However, in the interest of hearing you out, please tell us these conditions."

How was she so calm? I wanted to tear their idiotic contract into confetti and toss it back in their faces. Knives stabbed my skull as the gathered wolves' displeasure ricocheted through the mind link.

"Yes, Luna. We were a bit hasty at the meeting this morning in requesting an alternate liaison. The burrows are thrilled to have one of their own as the wolf shifter's luna." Frank beamed, and his beady eyes sparkled.

My skin crawled, and the hairs on my body rose. Something was wrong.

Sam spoke next. "This is an incredible opportunity for our two communities to come together—"

Monroe scoffed, cutting him off. "You are making this sound like it's an arranged marriage between two warring countries."

Sam smacked his palm on the table in excitement. "Exactly! That is the perfect description!"

We stared, slack-jawed and utterly speechless. They couldn't be so stupid as to lay claim to a wolf pack's luna, could they?

Oh, but they could.

"We've spoken at length, and although it is unorthodox to have a rabbit shifter mated to wolves, we can see how it could help create a better future for both species. At the ball, you were matched. This means you belong to Seth's fluffle. They have agreed that for the betterment of the burrows, they will still honor the match." Frank looked toward Seth and the rest of the pricks who'd humiliated my mate. His eyes shone with pride while my stomach churned with acid.

Now can I kill him? Rig snarled into the bond.

I should've said no, but I didn't want to. *Make it slow and messy.*

Yesss! Finally! Syrus's shout banged around in my head like a gong.

Rig's muscles tightened as he prepared to spring across the table.

No. The single word was a soft whisper in the mental link.

The three of us froze.

Did you hear that? I asked Rig and Syrus.

Yeah, Rig and Syrus answered.

Maybe it was one of the wolves? Syrus suggested.

No, I would recognize the voice. I know all my wolves.

With no small amount of effort, I followed the thin thread that created a link between my mind and the unknown speaker. My heart stopped.

Monroe? I asked hesitantly.

There was a brief pause, then came a soft *yes.*

It shouldn't be possible since we were two different

species, but somehow, she'd built a link to not only my mind, but to all three of ours.

Monroe said no. Back down, I ordered Rig.

Rig sat back, stunned at the knowledge our mate had spoken in the link.

All yours, my love. If you decide to start killing people, let Rig help, though. Otherwise, he'll sulk for weeks.

Monroe didn't respond to me. Her focus was on the gloating elders, and she was eyeing them like a predator does its prey.

It's about to go down.

Timber! Syrus cackled in the link.

Chapter TWENTY-FIVE

CILLIAN

"How do you expect that to work?" Monroe sounded almost amused.

My brain screamed *DANGER*.

I'd never had a mate before, or even time to date. But a primal survival instinct told me my mate was about to start sending souls to Hades, and that I should keep my mouth shut so I didn't catch any of her ire.

To my delight, Frank lacked any such survival instinct. "You will move back here with the boys, of course!"

"Oh, I see." Monroe's smile sent a shiver through me. "At the ball, Seth and his group didn't want to bond with me. They were willing to use my body for their entertainment, but they weren't willing to claim me as their bonded or the mother of their children. Which would have left me suffering from being bonded to them without having them feel the same toward me."

Sam spoke this time. "Ah, yes, but that isn't an issue now. You bonded with the three wolves during your first heat. It is unlikely you would bond with any other male after that. The boys have agreed to care for all your needs, including heats—"

He paused at the growls rumbling from our side of the table but then, like an idiot, continued, "They even agreed it would be wise to produce at least one child with you. Since you bonded to the wolves, it wouldn't be fair for your fluffle to be without a bonded, so they will be matched next spring. During your first heat, and when they are unavailable, you will be able to seek relief from the wolves. Hopefully, one of those breedings will produce offspring to help bring our two species even closer."

I was paralyzed and afraid that if I were to break free from it, I'd rampage through the burrows doing far more damage than the coyotes ever had. Rage pulsed from me in waves, and my pack felt it. Every wolf in the clearing crouched with their teeth bared, waiting for the command to attack.

Monroe's laugh pulled me from the dark edge I'd been teetering on. It was slightly unhinged, but that made it even more adorable.

"I knew the rabbit elders were out of touch with reality, but this is on a whole different level. Do you not realize how entitled you all sound right now?" Monroe wheezed.

"We don't appreciate your disrespect, Monroe. You should be grateful for all we've done for you instead of throwing it back in our face like a spoiled child." Spit flew from Frank's mouth.

"Grateful? For neglecting me? For depriving me of love? For ignoring my pleas for help because you are too blind to see the cruelty of the burrows' golden boys? Should I be grateful for being the laughingstock of the burrows at the ball just because your sons wanted to keep me as a pet for their amusement?" Monroe's chest heaved, and her eyes flashed.

"You"—Monroe made eye contact with each of the elders and their sons—"should all be grateful to the wolves! They have protected the burrows for years when they didn't have to. You found a soft-hearted alpha who felt protective toward our species, and you abused his good graces. They have never bullied us or treated us with disrespect. No, it is our community that thought they were too good to attend the same schools as the 'mutts.'"

Monroe snatched up the contract and held it up. "This is disgusting. There is no mutual respect in this contract. Only manipulation and greediness. Instead of using this second chance to be humble and show the wolves you appreciate what they've done for the burrows for all these years, you decided it was an opportunity to see how much more you could take from the wolves. You make me ashamed to be a rabbit."

Seth jumped up, leaning toward Monroe. "Bite your tongue! You know better than to speak to us like this. The wolves might have let you be the liaison, but you will do that job from the burrows so you can see what your people need."

"No. I will never spend another night in this prison." Monroe didn't scream, but her voice was firm.

"I'm sure these wolves enjoyed the experience of a female bunny in heat. They are probably still high on your taste and promising you the world. But you aren't that special, and they will get bored." He lowered his voice to a whisper, not that it mattered since every wolf there could hear him. "You can't trust those bloodthirsty mutts."

Rig was shaking with rage, and I was struggling to comprehend the level of duplicity and cruelty the elders were capable of. How had I been so blind to trust them? I'd used wolf resources to help their community grow and flourish, and they'd considered us nothing more than dogs?

Monroe stood, still maintaining her unbelievable dignity. "I trust them with my life. Far more than I'd ever trust any of you!"

"You are even more of an idiot than we thought. Do you think these wolves really care about you? You think they have the control to keep from snapping your neck? You need to get off your high horse and realize it's only a matter of time until you become a snack to one of those savage beasts," Seth hissed between his teeth.

Monroe clenched her jaw. Spinning on her heel, she walked confidently into the sea of angry wolves. One moment she was there, and the next, she vanished. My mouth fell open, and my eyes scanned the spot where she had stood.

Her sexy black dress lay on the ground.

The wolf closest to the dress, Reese, padded over and gingerly gathered the fabric in her mouth. Lifting the silk from the ground, she revealed a tiny ball of fluff.

I swallowed the lump in my throat.

It was one thing for her to feel the pull of a fated mate and trust Rig, Syrus, and myself, but it was another thing to trust wolves she'd never met. Her instincts should have made it impossible for her to shift into her bunny with so many wolves in the area. To a rabbit, it was a death wish.

We'd spent years protecting the rabbits, but they still saw us as monsters. Seth had degraded the wolves, calling us savages without control. Rather than argue, my mate was showing the wolves that she trusted them with her life.

She'd gone against instinct to stand up for the wolves and make her point in the most memorable way possible.

"*Awwww.* I forgot how cute she is as a bunny!" Syrus cooed, making a move to stand.

"Sit," I ordered. "Let her do this without us."

Reese dropped the gown and dropped to her belly in front of the gray bunny. Monroe hopped forward, touching noses with the charcoal wolf. Reese licked Monroe's face in greeting. The bunny huffed. Sitting on her hind feet, she used her tiny paws to wipe her wet fur.

Syrus snickered, no doubt remembering how disgruntled Monroe had been when he'd done that.

Once she'd cleaned her fur to her satisfaction, Monroe made her way through the wolves. It was quite the sight to watch the tiny rabbit hop her way between the wolves, with Reese prancing behind her like an overgrown, terrifying puppy.

Like dominoes, the wolves dropped to their bellies as the tiny rabbit came near, eager to greet her and show their respect. More than a few wolves' tails thumped happily on the ground, something they'd normally be teased over, but not this time. No one would tease a wolf for showing affection for their luna. Especially a luna who was this adorable.

Monroe seemed relaxed as she touched noses in greeting. Knives seemed to stab my skull at the intensity of the emotions pouring through the mental link from the pack. The tiny bunny had just wrapped an entire pack around her little paw in a matter of minutes.

Spinning around, she darted under Reese's body and nipped at her tail before taking off at top speed. Reese barked and took off after her.

What is she thinking? Is she trying to prove wolves will hunt rabbits? Rig growled through the link.

Syrus chuckled. *No, I think she's going to prove the exact opposite.*

The gray rabbit ducked under some of the wolves still standing and hopped over the ones who were lying on their bellies. Dodging and weaving, she led Reese on a wild chase through the pack. Wolves barked encouragement, and wanting to join in the game, they kept shifting positions, creating obstacles to slow Reese down.

Just as suddenly as she started it, Monroe screeched to a halt. Sides heaving from exertion, she flopped on the ground. Reese skidded to a halt, towering over the rabbit, breathing heavily and licking her lips to keep from drooling.

The rabbit shifters gasped. They believed they were about to see Monroe's death. After all, what wolf could get caught up in chasing prey and resist attacking them at the end of the hunt?

With a happy bark, Reese gently nipped Monroe's cotton-ball tail. Flopping onto the ground, the dark wolf stretched out alongside the bunny. Monroe wasn't quite done making her point. Pushing to her paws, she stared at the rabbit shifters who were watching wide-eyed. Thumping her back foot on the ground, she made sure she had their full attention.

Bouncing to Reese, she touched noses and then shoved her tiny head in a shocked Reese's mouth. Reese gagged and yanked her head away, coughing like she had a hairball.

The wolves barked and chuffed in laughter while the rabbit shifters looked stunned. The girl had been overly dramatic, but she'd made Monroe's point.

My mate had proven nothing would stop her from standing up for her pack. She'd also shown she had courage galore in that tiny body.

She'd already belonged to the wolves because she was the alpha's mate, but now she'd just earned their loyalty by her own merit.

I hated to think what would happen if anyone tried to touch her again.

Monroe hopped her way back to the table. Rig took off his jacket, gently laying it on the ground. The bunny scooted under it. Shifting back to her human body, she quickly pulled the jacket around her. Rig's leather jacket wrapped around her small frame twice.

Reese trotted over, dropping the luna crown at Monroe's feet with a soft whine.

"Thank you, friend." Monroe scratched behind Reese's ear.

Bending down, she grabbed the tiara and, with the confidence of a queen, she settled it on her head. It was slightly lop-sided, but with her glowing eyes and her untamed hair blowing around her face, she was the sexiest thing I'd ever seen.

Monroe stormed up to the table, bouncing up on the picnic table bench so she could glare down at the elders.

"I won't say this again. If you ever talk about my wolves like they are monsters again, you will need to relocate the burrows," she growled, which sounded adorable until the pack added their own growls to hers.

The elders gulped and looked nervously at each other.

Monroe's glowing amber eyes locked on me. "You said it is my decision regarding any agreement between our pack and the burrows, correct?"

I was lost in her eyes and nearly forgot to answer. "Yes."

She faced the elders. Raising her voice so the gathered shifters could hear, she gave her decision. "There will be no treaty. You've proven with your words that you never respected the wolves or appreciated their protection all these years. There is no reason for us to continue wasting resources."

Monroe looked past the elders at the rest of the rabbit shifters. "I've known very little kindness from anyone in the burrows other than my adoptive parents. However, I hope the entitled attitudes within this community are due to its poor leadership. If the burrows wished to seek a new agreement, I would consider it... but only after the current leaders are removed and new leaders have taken their place. There will be no exceptions."

She looked at the rabbit shifters scattered around the clearing. "If any rabbit in the burrows is being mistreated, please know that you can come to me for sanctuary. You don't have to stay here; you do have other options."

Monroe leapt off the table with an ease only a rabbit shifter could manage and started down the path toward the car, leaving everyone speechless.

"Alpha! You aren't going to let her talk to us like that, are you?" Elder Sam snarled.

I smirked. "You heard my luna. And she can do whatever she wants."

"Monroe! Where are you going?" Elder Frank screamed.

"I'm going HOME, and I'm taking all my wolves with me!" Without turning around, Monroe threw up both her hands, giving the rabbit shifters the middle finger salute.

Rig, Syrus, and I burst out laughing. It seemed our little

mate was coming out of her protective shell, and she was spicy.

Howls rang out as the wolves rushed to obey, disappearing into the woods the way they'd come. With a happy yip, Reese gathered Monroe's dress and high-heels.

"Take them to the pack house, please?" I called out.

With a nod of her head, Reese shot off into the woods.

"You're driving!" Rig tossed me the keys and took off after Monroe.

Chapter TWENTY-SIX

RIG

Watching my little mate strut away from the stunned elders was possibly the highlight of my entire life. Her sexy body, combined with her newfound attitude, already had my cock straining against my pants. But when the elders shouted after Monroe, she responded by throwing up her middle fingers… I was a goner.

"You're driving!" I tossed Cil the keys and took off at a run after the beauty wearing nothing but my leather jacket.

I caught up to her just as she reached the SUV and opened the back door. Grabbing her waist, I jumped in and moved to slam the door behind us.

"Oh!" Monroe gasped, clinging to me to steady herself.

My wolf was salivating after watching her play with the pack. If not for Cillian ordering us to let her do it on her own, I would have shifted and joined in the game of tag.

I'd held my wolf in check, but I was losing control. Lust clouded my brain. Watching her with Cillian in the office was the first time in my life I'd been jealous of my alpha.

All I could think about was my need to bury myself inside her, and hear her scream my name as she climaxed. I desperately wanted her to claw my shoulders and bite my skin. I'd seen the fire in her eyes in the conference room, and I wanted her to unleash it.

Syrus yanked the door handle from my hand. "There isn't a chance you're getting her all to yourself. Move."

I growled, reminding him I was beta and he couldn't order me around. But with Monroe's warm body in my arms, I decided I didn't care if he was there or not.

"Sit on the opposite side," I snarled, my voice the strange vibrato of my barely contained wolf.

I sat on the leather bench seat, and without a word, Syrus sat on the seat facing me. The SUV's interior was set up like a limousine. Its bench seats faced each other so we could conduct business while traveling to different locations.

"That was the hottest thing I've ever witnessed." I adjusted her so she straddled my lap, then rocked my hips up. "Feel what you did to me."

Monroe's eyes widened and then glowed with her own desire. She rolled her hips, rubbing against my length and moaning at the friction.

Chuckling, I slid my hands under my leather jacket to grip her hips. As she rocked on my lap, I ground her against my aching erection.

"It feels so good," Monroe whimpered.

"Mm-hmm," I agreed, my wolf pushing me to ignore any foreplay and breed our female.

"If you are going to make me keep my hands to myself, the least you could do is let me see her beautiful body," Syrus grumbled.

"Yes. Take it off," I growled. "I want you bare in my lap."

"What if someone sees?" she whispered, glancing nervously at the tinted SUV windows.

"They can't see in here. Now, take it off." Leaning in, I pressed my teeth into her neck. "Don't make me ask again."

Monroe gasped, hurrying to wiggle out of my jacket. It was so big on her small frame, it fell almost to her knees. She let it fall to the SUV's floor.

I sat back on the seat, taking my time and drinking in every inch of her naked body. She lifted her arms to cover her breasts.

"Don't," I growled.

Monroe slowly dropped her arms and met my eyes.

Dropping my pitch low, I praised her. "Good girl."

My mate's legs trembled, and the scent of her arousal grew stronger. I loved how responsive she was to us. My wolf was snarling for us to take her hard and fast, but I wanted to tease her just a little more.

I slipped a finger between her thighs, flicking it inside her tight channel.

"Rig," she whimpered.

Pulling my finger from her slick heat, I sucked it into my mouth. My chest rumbled at her sweet taste. "Delicious."

Monroe watched me, her eyes amber pools of lust.

"I'm going to take you so hard you won't be able to walk when I'm finished." My warning did nothing to cool the molten lava shimmering in her eyes. "If you don't want that, you need to tell me now."

"I want you, Rig," she purred.

"Kiss me," I ordered.

Monroe threw herself at my chest. Flinging her arms around my neck, she pressed her lips to mine and kissed me like she was starving.

I brushed my fingers down her soft skin, exploring every inch. She was making soft little mewls into my mouth as our tongues danced.

"Rig. Please," she begged, desperately working the buttons on my shirt.

I couldn't hold back any longer. Flicking open my pants, I freed my painfully stiff cock. I grabbed her hips and brought her down, impaling her on my length with a single hard stroke.

Monroe moaned, her nails clawing my chest as she tried to scramble away.

"Yes," I groaned.

I lifted her hips and brought her back down hard.

"Oh, Rig!" Monroe's mouth pressed to my neck, licking and sucking.

I rocked my hips, grinding against her clit; enjoying her sounds of pleasure.

When her nails dug tiny half-moons into my chest and shoulders, I could feel my release beginning to build. Wrapping my forearm around her waist, I pounded into her, driving us both closer to our orgasm.

Monroe clung to me, moaning and murmuring nonsense. Unable to resist, I sank my canines into the soft skin between her neck and shoulder. Pinned by my arm and my teeth, my beautiful mate was unable to get away—not that she was trying.

"Rig. I'm going to... to..." Monroe panted.

I growled, putting enough power into it to ensure Monroe's entire body vibrated.

"RIG!" Monroe screamed as I thrust hard enough to make her teeth clatter.

She came for me, her body clamping down on my length as the aftershocks of her climax rolled through her.

"Bite him, Puff. He likes the pain," Syrus murmured, his voice hoarse.

She didn't hesitate. Her teeth sank into my skin, and she raked her nails down my chest.

The orgasm tore through me with the force of a cyclone. I'd never come so hard in my life. My length twitched and jerked inside her, the base beginning to swell. I could pull out now, and she wouldn't be stuck on me. But I didn't want this to end.

Grabbing her hips, I forced the swelling base inside her, locking us together. Monroe bit me a second time as the friction of my swollen cock rubbed her just right and coaxed a second orgasm from her.

Wrapping both arms around her, I slumped back on the bench seat, pulling her with me. I spent the rest of the ride back to our home licking and nuzzling my mate as she cuddled against my chest. She was perfect.

I'd never been so content.

Chapter TWENTY-SEVEN

MONROE

I t had been about two weeks since the big showdown in the burrows. My heat had ended, and I'd managed not to breed my mates to death. Which was good since, heat or no heat, I couldn't get enough of them.

Sadly, with my pain gone, they'd needed to catch back up on things at the office. They hadn't been comfortable leaving me alone, so they'd been taking turns staying at home with me.

It was adorably sweet, but I'd been cooped up too much the past few weeks and needed an outing. It had taken more than a little convincing, but the guys finally agreed to let me have a girls' day with Reese.

In her human form, Reese was the opposite of her dark-furred wolf. She wore her blonde hair in a bouncy bob that suited her bubbly personality perfectly. Her skin was paler than mine, and was dotted with freckles that added to her sweet girl-next-door vibe.

"This place has the best margaritas and salsa. You're going to love it, Ro!" Reese's sea-foam green eyes sparkled. Yanking open the restaurant door, she practically dragged me inside.

I laughed, loving her enthusiasm. "I can't wait!"

My life had changed so much in such a short amount of time. Not only did I have three sexy mates, I had a friend— and not the imaginary kind I'd had growing up.

The restaurant was dimly lit, giving it a cozy feel. The tall-backed wooden booths were painted in cheerful hues of reds, blues, greens, and yellows. Reese led me to one of the booths, playfully shoving me onto one of the cushions before sliding onto the cushion across from me.

We'd barely sat down before a sweet older lady came to take our order. Reese opened her mouth to order, but was cut off by our waitress. "Reese, if you're planning to murder my ears with what you call Spanish, I'll kick you out."

They clearly knew each other, because both women were fighting a smile. "But Stella, how else am I supposed to practice my Spanish?" Reese's eyes turned to dark pools as she gave Stella puppy eyes.

"Ay mi hijita! Don't give me those eyes. It won't work. Go use Duolingo like everyone else!" Stella playfully smacked Reese on the back of the head with the plastic menus.

Placing one of the menus in front of me, Stella set the

other in front of Reese. "I will be back to get your orders in a few minutes."

"She's the best!" Reese whispered after Stella was out of earshot.

"Of course I am!" Stella called over her shoulder.

"Is she a werewolf?" I whispered. I hadn't smelled a wolf, but her hearing was far better than a human's hearing.

"No. She's Latina." Reese grinned and answered as though it made perfect sense. "Nothing gets by her."

I smiled back, my heart warming at the obvious affection between the two.

We spent the next few minutes looking over the menu and ordering our food. Stella set two baskets of warm tortilla chips and a bowl of chunky salsa on the table, and we dug in.

Between mouthfuls of food, Reese chatted about everyone in the pack. It was as though she was determined to catch me up on a lifetime of wolf shifter gossip in a single hour.

And I loved every second of it.

"Well, isn't this cute?"

I recognized his voice before I looked up.

Seth.

My stomach twisted, and bile rose in my throat.

Seth pushed into the booth beside me, while Zane crowded in beside Reese. My blonde bestie growled, and I thought she was going to attack him. Instead, she snatched the salsa and chips away, guarding them with her arms. At least she had her priorities straight.

Malcolm, Tom and Jordy pulled up chairs at the end of the table. I was squished between Seth and the wall. They'd blocked us in.

"I see your jail keepers finally let you out of their sight." Seth smirked. "A mistake on their part."

Reese's growls turned to laughter. "You guys are idiots to even be talking to Monroe." She scooped up some salsa with a chip. "You're all going to die."

Was she crazy? She was a wolf shifter, but these guys weren't small and we were outnumbered. My gaze darted around the room, searching for pack mates. My heart sank. The restaurant was empty other than our table, and a table with humans on the opposite side of the restaurant.

Seth *tsk*-ed. "Oh, I'm sure you've already alerted the alpha. Unfortunately, there were rumors of coyotes on pack territory, and he took his strongest wolves to deal with the threat. Even if he runs at full speed, we will be gone before he gets here, mutt."

It was his name-calling that flipped my crazy switch. I straightened my spine and stopped pressing myself into the wall. "Don't call her mutt."

"Look at you getting all protective, *luna*." He emphasized the last word, letting me know he thought the title was a joke.

"Just say the word, bestie." Reese popped a chip in her mouth and licked the salsa from her fingers.

Carrot cake!

Reese was as crazy as Rig. Did I just attract the slightly unhinged?

I needed to defuse the situation. "Seth, this isn't a fight you want. Go back to the burrows. The only reason Cillian hasn't decimated the burrows, is because I asked him to just ignore the rabbit shifters. He isn't going to be happy when he finds out. And he sure as heck won't be in a generous mood if you're here when he arrives."

Seth grabbed my chin in a bruising grip. Yanking my mouth toward his, he stopped just shy of our lips touching. "You ruined our lives. And now you've whored yourself out to the wolves, letting them take what was always meant to be mine."

I froze, years of trauma and cruelty at his hands flashing through my mind. Reese didn't wait for my order, and lunged across the table. She might be in her human form, but she would still be stronger than a human female.

Rabbit shifters had one advantage over wolves. We were slightly faster. Zane used that to his advantage. Grabbing the dull knife on the table, Zane slammed it between her ribs.

"No!" I shrieked as Reese hit the food covered tabletop. Drinks toppled, dishes cracked, and her blood mixed with the salsa spreading across the table.

Out of the corner of my eye, I caught sight of Stella rushing the humans out of the back of the restaurant. Relieved they would be safe, I focused back on Seth.

Rage like nothing I'd ever known erupted in my chest and burned in my veins. They'd never wanted me, but now that I wasn't their problem, they wanted to take everything from me.

I'd made a friend, and now she lay bleeding on the table. All because she'd tried to protect me. I was her luna, and no one touched my wolves.

Using the same speed Zane had used when he stabbed Reese, I snatched the broken margarita glass. Bouncing off my seat and onto the table, I slammed it into Zane's face. I wasn't sure what I hit, but his screams of pain told me it was probably important.

Seth tried to stop me, but I was a rabbit shifter too... and I had years of rage fueling me. Spinning around on the slick surface of the table, I kick out hard with both feet.

There was an ominous cracking sound when my boots connected with his ribcage. I made a mental note to thank Rig for picking the cute and deadly combat boots.

Seth coughed and wrapped his arms around his chest. I wasn't done, though. Sinking both my hands into his hair, I yanked his head down. Hard.

There was a crack as his skull connected with the corner of the table and his body went limp.

OH CRAPPITY CRAP CRAP!

I hadn't meant to kill him... or maybe I had?

Help! I shrieked into the mental link with my mates, not sure they could even hear me. I could barely manage to connect when they were sitting beside me, it was unlikely they could hear me from miles away.

Malcolm, Jordy, and Tom shoved out of the chairs to catch Seth as he slumped to the floor, blood pouring from his head and mouth.

My head snapped up when Stella came roaring from the

kitchen, waving a butcher's knife in one hand and a pan in the other. She wasn't coming to mess around, but I didn't want her caught in the middle of this.

Reese groaned, trying to sit up. I needed to get us out of here before Seth's little gang turned their attention back to us.

"Stella! Help me get Reese." Stella changed course, having been ready to pummel Malcolm with the cast iron pan.

We looped our arms under Reese and rushed into the kitchen and toward the backdoor. Shoving it open, we came face to face with a vicious pack of wolves. My ears rang with angry snarls and howls as they poured into the restaurant.

Stella and I half-dragged, half-carried Reese a safe difference from the chaos.

"Are you okay?" Reese whispered.

The adrenaline was wearing off and tears streamed down my cheeks. "Why are you worried about me? I'm fine! You're dying!"

Reese's giggle turned into a groan. "I'm a wolf shifter, I'll heal. You aren't getting rid of me that quick."

On impulse, I threw my arms around her neck, squeezing her tight.

"You were epic, Luna." She patted my back while Stella fussed over Reese's injuries.

Then my other worry rose to the surface. "Reese, I think I killed him!"

"Nah. His heart was still beating. Unfortunately, he'll live—"

A roar of fury tore through the air and Rig's wolf blurred across the parking lot and into the restaurant.

"Nevermind." Reese shrugged, then winced. "Rig is definitely going to kill him."

Chapter TWENTY-EIGHT

MONROE

Cillian and Syrus showed up moments after Rig. Both wolves rushed to me, shifting into their human forms to check me for injuries. Stella let loose with a rapid-fire string of Spanish.

"What is she saying?" I asked Reese, worried Stella wasn't going to be able to handle the knowledge that shifters existed.

"Girl, my Spanish sucks," Reese snickered. "But I recognize enough words to know it is your mates' bodies that caught her attention, not the fact that two wolves just turned into men. I think she's wishing she were twenty years younger."

"We heard you in the link. We thought you were hurt." Cillian's chest heaved, and he pressed his forehead to mine.

Reese guffawed. "Heck no! Your sweet little luna has

you fooled into thinking she's a scared rabbit. She's an assassin ninja bunny."

My mates gave her twin looks of confusion, and Syrus moved to check her stab wound.

"Monroe, if you are truly okay, I'm going to go make sure the pack doesn't go on a rampage. You didn't just call us... you called the pack. Between that and the smell of blood, they are going to have to fight their wolves to regain control." Cillian stood, but hesitated.

"Go! I'm fine. Make sure our wolves are okay. Shoo." I motioned for him to go. "Syrus can get us home."

Reluctantly, Cillian took a step backward before turning on his heel and shifting into his wolf.

"Let's go home." Syrus stood and held out his hand to help me to my feet.

"Syrus, what about Reese and Stella? We can't let Stella back in there until it's clean and everything that's being destroyed is replaced."

"We'll take them home with us. Reese's brothers are in the fray, and we aren't leaving her alone." Syrus bent and scooped Reese into his arms.

"Stella, we need you to come with us." I looped my arm through hers. "Okay?"

The older woman hesitated, but finally nodded. "You two are a mess and I have questions. Let's go." Untying her apron, she tossed it to me. "But have your man put this on. My old heart can't handle your man candy."

I laughed and quickly tied the pink ruffled apron

around Syrus' waist. He looked like a photo from a buff firefighter calendar. It was absurd, but also sexy as heck.

Giggling, I smacked Syrus on the butt. "Let's go home, Betty Cocker!"

I SIGHED, SNUGGLING TIGHTER AGAINST SYRUS' chest. This had been the longest day in the history of days.

After we arrived home, Syrus had settled Reese in a guest room. Stella had hurried to help her shower and bandage her wound. While Stella had tended to Reese, I'd gone to take my own shower, eager to wash the blood, salsa and sticky margarita from my skin.

Now we were in the living room, sipping hot cocoa, while Stella bustled around our kitchen. Incredible scents wafted through the room.

"Is she cooking or rearranging the cabinets?" I whispered.

"Both. Cooking seems to be her way of working through anxiety. Plus, she wasn't impressed by our bachelor house-keeping. I think we've been adopted," Syrus chuckled.

"I hope so! What I ate today at her restaurant was delicious!"

Reese laughed. "I'm going to be here for dinner every night, if that's the case!"

The front door swung open, and Cillian stormed inside. "He won't freaking listen to me!"

"Who won't?" I asked.

My question was answered when Rig trotted in behind him, his wolfy tail wagging happily.

"DROP IT," Cillian ordered, pushing enough alpha command into his words that even I felt it.

Rig rumbled a complaint and dropped the stuffed toy he was carrying.

"What is that?" Syrus squinted at the toy.

"Not what. You mean *who*," Cillian hissed. "Rig! I didn't mean to drop him in here! Take him back outside!"

Reese burst into laughter. "He brought you a rabbit!"

"What?!" I squeaked, looking closer.

A sinking feeling filled the pit of my stomach when I recognized the rabbit's pelt. "Seth."

Reese clutched her sides, howling with laughter. "Your mate just brought you a dead rabbit as a gift like a fricking kitty cat."

"He's dead?" I croaked.

"Yes, oh wait. Maybe not—"

The rabbit leapt to his paws and bounded across the floor toward the kitchen, hoping to escape the wolves.

Stella's shout was followed by the racket of pans being thrown around the kitchen.

"Get him, Stella!" Reese screamed encouragement.

Rig barked and scrambled to join the chaos. His nails couldn't get traction, and he slid across the hardwood floors, crashing into walls and furniture.

184

The doorbell rang, adding one more thing to the poop storm that was currently our home. Cillian threw up his hands.

"Rig! Catch the rabbit and take him to the jail with the rest of his friends!" Cillian roared after my bloodthirsty mate.

I started to get up, but Cillian motioned for me to stay. "You rest. I'll handle it."

Flinging open the door, and clearly prepared to scare off any would-be visitors, Cillian snarled. "You best not be from the rabbit council. I'm really not in the mood today."

"Um, no. I mean, yes," a soft feminine voice said from outside.

I scrambled off Syrus' lap and headed to the open door. Ducking under Cillian's arm, I came face-to-face with a blue eyed, blue-haired rabbit shifter.

"You aren't from the council." I bit my lip, trying to remember if I'd ever seen her. "I don't think I've ever seen you in the burrows."

She twisted her hands together. "No, I'm not from your old burrow. My name is Ellora. I'm from the Greenbriar burrow in Oregon."

I held out my hand. "Nice to meet you, Ellora. I'm—"

"Oh! I already know who you are! I bet every bunny in the US knows who you are!" Ellora took my hand, flashing me a small smile.

"What do you mean?" Cillian questioned.

Ellora's eyes shot up to meet his and her smile fell

away. "Monroe is the bunny who runs with wolves. She's turned our world upside down."

Dizziness washed through me. I didn't want to be known across the US. All I wanted was to enjoy my pack and be left alone by those who'd hurt me in my old burrow.

"Someone recorded the meeting in the clearing and leaked the video. You were incredible, and I realized I didn't have to accept a role I'd been forced into either. At the end, you told the rabbits that they had other options and they could come to you." Ellora glanced nervously behind her. "I know you were talking to your old burrow, but I hoped if I could get here, you'd help me escape too."

My heart banged in my chest, and I met her tear-filled eyes. I saw the same pain I'd gone through shimmering in their brilliant blue depths.

"Was it your bonded?" I asked, already knowing the answer.

She nodded. "Except I wasn't able to run before my heat hit. They don't love me, they just want me to give them heirs and take care of their every need. I couldn't stay any longer, so I ran."

Reaching out, I took her hand and led her into the house.

"Of course we'll help." I gave her a hug as she sank to the floor, sobbing. "You're not alone."

I looked up at Cillian, pleading with him to agree with me.

"You are safe here, Ellora. I've already sent a message

through the mental link that you are to be protected as a member of the pack. I'm glad you are here. Monroe has been cut off from the local burrow and that is hard for any shifter. Please stay as long as you wish." Cillian bent and pressed a soft kiss to my lips.

Hope and joy burst inside me. With the help of my wolves, our little town could become a safe haven for bunny shifters.

I had loving mates, a loyal pack, a best friend, and now... *I had a purpose.*

ABOUT SEDONA ASHE

Sedona Ashe doesn't reserve her sarcasm for her books; her poor husband can tell you that her wit, humor, and snarky attitude are just part of her daily life. While she loves writing paranormal shifter reverse harem novels, she's a sucker for true love, twisted situations, and wacky humor.

Sedona lives in a small town at the base of the Great Smoky Mountains in Tennessee. She and her husband share their home with their three children, adorable pup, five cats, an arctic fox, chickens, several crazy turkeys, two chubby frogs, an emu with happy feet, and over a hundred reptiles. When she isn't working, she enjoys getting away from the computer to hike, free dive, travel, study languages, and capture places and animals in her photography. She has a crazy goal of writing a million words in a year, and spending six months exploring Indonesia.

You can find more information about the author and her books here:

www.authorsedonaashe.com

www.instagram.com/sedonaashe
www.facebook.com/sedonaashe

Made in United States
North Haven, CT
23 May 2023

36896599R00118